Krishna Vasudev

an illustrated novel

Alok Bajpai

illustrator

Pranoy Basak

editor/translator

Ishita Sehgal

vaniprakashan.com

Paperback First Edition : 2024

Yatra Books is an imprint of Vani Prakashan Group

Head Office

4695, 21-A, Daryaganj, New Delhi-110 002, India
Phone : +91 11 23273167, 23275710

Registered Bookstores and Offices

Ashok Rajpath, Patna - 800 004, Bihar
Coffee House Campus, Mahatma Gandhi Marg, Allahabad -211 001, Uttar Pradesh
Mahatma Gandhi Antarrashtriya Hindi VishwaVidyalaya, Wardha-442 001, Maharashtra
36-A, Shakespeare Sarani, Near Rani Birla Girls College, Kolkata -700017, West Bengal

sales@vaniprakashan.in
vaniprakashan@gmail.com

Krishna Vasudev : An Illustrated Novel
by Alok Bajpai

ISBN : 978-93-6287-536-5
An Illustrated Novel

Printed at City Press, Delhi-110095

Vani Prakashan's signature motif is created by Artist Maqbool Fida Husain

Grateful to
Krishna himself,
and to all those,
who love him

Preface

Mythology is an important basic of human cognitive development across all human cultures. The myth of hero is universal, but Indian mythology surpasses rest for the deitification of the hero. The hero turns to God and all acts are considered miracles that further feed the myth. Dashavatar, the incarnation of Lord Vishnu, adds to this theory. But an important fact is often ignored, each Avatar is limited by the body and mind it appears in.

The heroes of the epic Ramayana and Mahabharata, Ram and Krishna or gods in our times are often at the centre of blind worship. But gods are often difficult to follow because their acts are not considered to be human. On the contrary, if we try to look at them as humans who could use their capacity to the fullest and self actualise themselves, physically or mentally, we can learn the process and parts of divinity and it can be open to most.

This book in autobiographical form narrates the life of the blue God Krishna and how he was led by his intelligence and genius mind.

— Dr. Alok Bajpai

Illustrator's note

This work by Dr. Alok Bajpai titled - **'Krishna Vasudev',** hands out a very different outlook of Krishna, the 'blue god', whom we have heard, read and seen in a specific way. This work is a result of mere interpretation as to what might have happened actually at that time, as the incidents and stories we here in our mythology seems fanatasical to a great extent.

As an illustrator, I had to completely change my outlook and the image of what the society has shown me of Krishna till now. The major challenge was to show him as a 'human Krishna' rather than a 'God Krishna' but still maintain the character - 'Krishna'. In simple words, the demand was to change the image of Krishna while still maintaing the character. Due to this reason, the blue skin of Krishna, that we normally see everywhere, has been replaced with normal human-like colour to eradicate his 'divine' look and hand him the more 'human' look. Another element to notice is that in almost every illustration, Krishna can be seen adorned with a peacock feather necklace instead of a feather being attached to his hair. The concept here is that the peacock feather has been used as symbol of Krishna before being just an ornament. As to a realistic approach, obviously he must not be having the peacock feather attached to his head all the time but a necklace with a pendant can be and in many cases worn all the time. There are specific incidents and stories in the wiriting ahead that have been narrated using the 'realism' approach. Mostly those have been choosen to be illustrated to provide a visual image in the minds of the reader that explains what the whole incident may have looked like.

In all, this whole project has been an interesting one to work upon and the different outlook of Dr. Alok Bajpai made it quite challenging in a fun way. An important point to end with - this whole work including the writing and based on it the illustration is a mere interpretation, a different realistic outlook and a different kind of imagination. I hope you enjoy experiencing the Krishna that we have presented to you different than the conventional ways and you discover the idea of Krishna rather than an individual.

—Pranoy Basak

Editor / Translator's note

Translation from one language to another can be in spirit or literal. Especially for minds who think and work bilingually. It oftens becomes a metaphorical exercise. More so, when it is about the enigma named Krishna; the God, the complete man whose life is an important part of the collective unconscious of an Indian mind. Translating this book from Hindi to English was like revisiting Krishna's life and my own Krishna kept jumping into this work. However, I had to contain my impulse so that Dr Alok Bajpai's hindi version is not layered by my interpretations. But I am glad that we know Krishna in the same way.

Hope you find your Krishna in this effort.

—Ishita Sehgal

I am known as *Vrishni Kumar—Krishna Vasudeva.* I spent a small period of 100 years on this planet, some 3-4 thousand years ago. The ever flowing nature of time, turned these 100 years into small tremors of time and space.

Even now when I try to remember the time gone, I wish to come back. But alas, I don't have the fate of rebirth in my own hands. This can only happen when humankind creates situations that are beyond their own will.

The desire became stronger when I heard about the part of the planet called *Bharat;* it was divided even then. *Mathura, Paanchal, Magadh, Hastinapur* and many other kingdoms like these were caught amidst gruesome war. The egoistic and all powerful kings were at each other's throats. I too had established a *Dwaraka* far away, but what other choice did I have ? My power to bind with love was beginning to fail.

But now it feels like, maybe, man today would be less egoistic and selfish. My urge to prove this true has put me in a grave peril which has resulted in me writing this. I am writing this because today's man doesn't try to listen.

My time on earth was an attempt to live life in a way that helped people live happily. If only I knew unity, love and bliss would turn out to be this troublesome and hard to achieve, I would have searched for alternative paths.

I was shocked to hear that I, Krishna, was a god on earth. In my time on earth, a lot of people tried to make me god and all I did, was labelled as miracles. I tried hard to convince them that it was all human but probably their mental doubt and low self-confidence made them transfer the cause and effect of every incident and decision on my person making me divine. But I was forced with my habits to indulge in fight and not flight whatever the result would be. They were actually scared of their inaction that made my action look like a miracle.

The mob that tried turning me into a god scared me then and it scares me even now. I was thinking that the human race must have sharpened their wits and must have calmed their minds by now. But what I saw was the opposite. Bharat has temples in my name, wherever I stepped became a pilgrimage and what I spoke became The Gita.

Instead of solving problems, people waste time searching for me. There have been so many men of action like me, Christ, Shiv, Buddha, Ram, Muhammad, Gandhi and they are being turned into Gods as well. And as if this isn't enough cause man is still manufacturing new gods. The one who turns lies into the truth, turns misery into hope turns from man to god. But most of them are caught in an ego trip, just like Hitler.

But whichever and whatever story is revered, it is not about the common man. These stories aren't about what the common man does, what he thinks or what he dreams of. These stories are about kings, powerholders, and Gods. And now my biggest doubt is of this being the biggest lie, that the man in power is actually thinking about the common and the downtrodden. The gap between Kings and the common man is filled with ego and power. Every man is stuck in this race, of knowledge, money or power. All I wanted was to be a part of the people, connect with them and I did, from *Gokul* to *Dwarka,* but when my story was told I was turned from the common to the elite. All I want to tell you today is that the ones who are worshipped are just like you, weak, scared and caught in their own mental turmoil. Someone is a Suyodhana or Duryodhan.There feet always trample the others. Man will mature the day when he finds god by his own brain and knowledge and not by searching for gods made by others. But why search? To change thoughts is suffering, sometimes even sorrow. But to live in the influence and aura of the others is easy. As soon as god exits, the aura disappears and the mind is back to misery.

What did this poison do to me ?

I was like everyone else in my childhood, always full of myself on my success, but I became conscious real soon. Those who think that God is away from all of this, are wrong. The human mind is the same, one has to rise and fall multiple times to rise again to become a god. And the ones who are asking to be worshipped are illusory.

But this path is filled with dangers, if we want to rise above the human mind and create a sense of equanimity, everybody is worthy of compassion. This vision can intensify ego and thus it needs knowledge. Not the borrowed knowledge but a deep dive into the mind onto the finest division of time where self gets inflated, the vision has to be altered.

True love and compassion can be without the self. Going beyond it is the only struggle and obstcle.

I could do this only through incessant struggle, even when I knew about the three ages, but that happened only when I could pierce through the human mind. People used to begin from the top, trapped in their own reflections, I used to walk in sync with time, from the bottom, from zero to one. Past and future do not hold any importance in that moment. *Yog, Drastha, Tathagat, Purush- Prakriti,* the path of god opens at that subtle level, for me as well as you.

This is my account.

Who made this story famous and when remains a question. The first person to come to mind is the great poet Vyas. Since my departure from earth he wrote 'Jaya' where he talked about the ghastly war and the war that people named as the Mahabharata. Vyas only wrote about my role in the struggles but who turned me into a divine energy is unknown.

The truth is that since my birth, crises and struggles of duties pulled me towards them. I don't know if it was my inner calling or people in despair that kept me going. The question of me walking towards troubles or whether troubles invited me, is still alive. Whether people were consoled or awed by my actions was beyond my control. I have been told that my life had been chronicled in the Harivansh Puran and the Bhagvat Katha and my actions were termed as leela. Some great man even found a mention of me in the Chandogya Upanishad, which was written years before me. Was that even me ? But I don't remember. Maybe there was a different Krishna before me.

Who knows what I remember about my life could be like some other Krishnas somewhere doing exactly what I was doing. All these stories began to be associated with me.

There is not a singular Krishna, there could be multiple Krishna with different bodies but similar thoughts !

Butitisnotsureif thingsactuallychanged.Scienceprovided man with equal amounts of brain and strength, yet man still has faith, faith in the God that will solve all their struggles, by providing them with what they need and by ending their egos.

I spent my entire life trying to avoid these feelings and I kept telling man that I was one with them, the only difference being that I was awake and they were asleep.

By telling my story today, future Krishnas could be saved and I want to tell you the reasons and the results. I want to throw light on my life.

Life prospers in the shadows of death. When the heart begins to beat in a mother's womb, life gears up to rush towards the mouth of death.The life force and the unconscious mind knows this and tries to stay alive. The thought of this controls man and all the other deeds are the steps to reaching immortality.

Some people sacrifice themselves, some build castles, some sing and some through power and kingship try and keep themselves alive.

But, if death keeps visiting you then the choice between fighting or extinction is inevitable. When a child was incapable of protecting himself, I was facing attacks and kept protecting myself in return. At least that's what I remember! But as soon as I got my mind under control, the tensions of the others around me made me fight for their erasure or ease of others.

The attempt to save myself turned into me saving my village and my lineage, for both me and Balram, this became the ongoing struggle of our lives.

The story of me killing the demons in my childhood, are not the physical demons instead their nature and actions made them demons . Any strong man could have defeated them, they only had to keep their calm and fears away.

The demons had powers to capture man in a web of lies which usually put the person's mind in doubt and thus paving the way for evil to prosper. That is why when Balram and I killed such monsters, as children, greatness was heaped upon us and people ran to us in times of trouble.

Now that I think about it, I feel it wasn't a great feat. We were young, unaware of fear and that is why demons and their acts felt like games and attacking them became our instinct, like all animals. We had nothing to lose and winning was the reward. And both of us had this art of play. Balram used to get angry easily but I had the ability to stop him. The way to defeat the enemy was to tire him and hurt the ego which led to the demons' self defeat. We kept playing and by the time we faced our uncle Kansa, we had learnt the art.

Keeping non-violence over violence and the power of tolerance, the capacity to stay in the battle ground, these skills are enough to defeat the enemy. We had to take up arms to stay in the field. Centuries later this same struggle revisited the soil of *Bharat*, to overthrow the British, there was another Mohan who was born, Mohandas Gandhi. This time around he didn't even pick up weapons but he defeated the enemy with his inner strength otherwise when does a pinch of salt shake the throne!

My life story has been narrated multiple times in different ways, so repeating that would be boring. Instead, I will

tell you what I think about my life. Perhaps this helps people in fixing some old mistakes and helps them in making their lives better.

What is Bharat like today is not what is important. What is important is whether mankind has evolved or not. Does hate, jealousy, lust, ego and greed still control the mind ? I will tell you about my life and you can think about yours..

Searching for myself, I got lost on this earth. Who is Krishna ?

This simple question has unleashed a plethora of such questions.

Someone has turned me into a dream and for some I am a myth. When asked, most of them pointed towards an idol of me and the rest towards the Gita. (I think I said this to Arjuna, before the war)

When I observed the idol deeply, I could not recognize myself.

Chakra, the peacock's feather, the flute were very dear to me but I did not roam around with them. And my idols, somewhere I was a kid, somewhere on a chariot and some places the King of Dwaraka. And above all of this my infinite names.I doubt if I was even called Krishna. Chakradhari, mukutdhari, natvar, Thakur, Liladhar, Madhav, Ghanshyam and what not. It's not that I am not used to these names. But every time someone calls me by a new name I ask them, and I ask you too- whether you are looking for me or parts of me ? And where are you looking for me and why ?

The world has developed and science has reached new heights but I am shocked that you don't think of new things about the man you made into God. The same old demeanor, no new stories, no new miracles. Why pray to such an old god ?

Today I will talk to you not like a god but like a human who knew the struggle of being a human and has tried to live to his full potential. This process is Krishna Vasudev himself. The route from human to god is not on the outside, but on the inside of your mind, and if I could traverse on this route, anyone can.

People turned me into god from human and I am taking a reverse journey...

Let me tell you an incident. After the war, the war that you call the Mahabharata, I was returning to *Dwarka*. For many years my mind was away from home, I was worried about *Aryavarta* and politics. Children grew up and we had grown old. On the way we took shelter in the hermitage of *Rishi Utang*.

These travels were a part of my life. None of them took me back to the old route. What was left was left forever. From *Gokul* to *Mathura, Mathura* to *Dwarka* and from *Dwarka* to *Kurukshetra,* the travels had to stop now. Whatever the travel is, the path is always fraught with dangers.

We were just about to enter the desert, with the entire *Yadav* clan from *Mathura* when a learned man told us a difficult but a naturally easier route. We reached the west coast by walking through the forest, saving ourselves from *Jarasandh.* My names became famous because of my deeds, I am sure you know *Ranchod das* (one who leaves the battleground). People started remembering me by the acts I performed in a particular geographical area.

Even if I left, the battle ground never left Krishna, even in that great escape. The citizens of Mathura left the shadows of the desert deaths and reached the mountains and were on the way to the jungles of Gir.

Dau and I stayed back with a few *Yadava* soldiers to distract *Jarasandh.*

Dau said "*Kanha,* you stay behind, I will end this problem for once and all." In a small battle, *Dau* and *Jarasandh* came across each other but I stopped *Dau*, why I did that, I still don't know. Later, *Jarasandh* had followed us to *Dwarka.*

At that time to run away I created a sand storm and climbed the mountains with *Dau.* I could have caught the rest of the entourage on the other side. The other side had a jungle and I had burned the jungle down to stop the army. Burning jungles had turned out to be a job for me.

Jarasandh stopped in that moment but he wasn't an ordinary warrior. He had called a friend of his from the far west country of Greece. (Yavan) As if the men in Aryavart were less, that they had to call foreigners too ! But the hunger for land and kingdoms was the way of life for them. He reached *Mathura* with three lakh soldiers and when he did not find me there, he lost his calm and entered the jungle like an arrow shot straight from a bow.

In between this our entourage had one mission to go far away from there and reach *Somnath* from where through water they could reach *Dwarka. Dau* and I were roaming around, like it was a game for us. The enemy had eyes on us and the people of *Mathura* were safe.

No one has seen the future, it comes in a blink of an eye. The day I met my people in the jungle and I was just about to enter the dream land after having food,when I heard a voice that said, "Wake up, It isn't time yet."

I thought gods had arrived. In my mind all I could think about were *Jarasandh* and *Kalyavan.* But instead it was *Dau*, ready with the plough on his shoulder. Looking at him even in those troublesome times, standing like that made me laugh.

"Dau, where are you headed? You used to look like this

when we used to farm as kids. Where are the farms here ?"

"Not fields, with this plough, I will bury their heads in this very jungle, I have run enough because of you."

My sleep ran away in a jiffy. *Dau* was red with anger.

"*Dau*, no. I am not running. Their death is making them run. But what happened?"

"*Kalyavan* is three days away from here, all these people are tired and none of them can walk any further. We have to keep them safe." *Dau* said.

"What is your advice, *Dau* ?"

Dau used to walk behind me, and I used to try not to trouble him but troubles used to walk ahead of me. And one day *Dau* used to get fed up and he wanted to deal with the problems in his own way: by eliminating the enemy. I used to let him deal with it in his own way, only if the results were not detrimental to us.

But *Kalyavan* wasn't such a problem. He was a foreigner and I had no clue of his powers and I did not want to put *Dau* in danger.

"*Dau*, you are needed here. These people will be calmer with your presence, they don't trust me that much, you stay here I will take satyki with me and go.If I don't return in three days you leave with everyone."

"*Kanha*, you alone..?"

"*Dau*, I am not alone, you are there, do you remember *Kaaliya*?"

Dau took a deep breath and kept his plough down and said "Go and free him."

I called Satyaki and both of us disguised ourselves, carrying blankets, sticks and food. We went back on the same route from where we came.

I had to hide my form, my dark colour so I left all my symbols behind.I hadn't received the Sudarshan yet. Satyki had hidden the sharpened weapons. He could read signs even in the dark. We didn't have to go too far, one and a half days had gone by and we were searching near the waterside. On a hill we saw some movement, and we understood at once.

As soon as we climbed down, we saw the large army; tall and fair soldiers. Satyki and I looked at each other and we only had one thought- We got saved. We wouldn't have survived a day in front of this army. In between some tents, a man was sitting under a tree, with his hand on a sword, drinking from a cup. He was *Kalyavan.*

I was really jealous of Kalyavan's build and strength and at the same time I was proud, because he was my enemy. If it would have been a different time, I would have tried to learn more about him, his land, the culture of Greece. But today was not the day of learning, it was the day of surviving. But I did not want to fight him without

knowing anything about him. He hadn't yet declared his animosity to me, he had just followed me. At the same time I was impressed by him because in an unknown land, where he knew no one, he was following someone. This could be possible only because he was mentally strong.

I told Satyki to stay hidden and to keep an eye on me. I reached right outside their camp and the soldiers tried taking me to Kalyavan. But, I was stubborn about meeting him there because I told them that I had news about Krishna. I did this, because I wanted to keep the escape routes open. I sat right there, waiting. In a short while, Kalyavan was standing in front of me, and I was reaching somewhere near his shoulder.

"Who are you ?"

"I have news about Krishna."

"But he is your own, why are you telling me about him ?"

I could not think of an answer at that moment

"Because Krishna has troubled me a lot, he has taken all my calmness."

He looked at me for a while and said "Tell me."

"If you promise to give him my life as alms, I will make you meet him."

Till now my face was covered with a blanket and now he asked me to show my face.

There was no way out, once I removed the blanket, he could not recognize me but one of his servants whispered something in his ear.

He turned and faced the other side, I took a step back.

There was silence for a while. My sixth sense could feel the danger coming.

And suddenly the volcano erupted !

He screamed "Krishna, you lied to me!"

He said "Start remembering death or surrender and earn a new life, as I have said before. I hope you are not foolish to fight in front of this vast army."

" Kalyavan, I have no enmity for you but you want to fight with me ? For your friend? Just like I am doing this for my family."

I emphasized on what I said "Become friends with me and leave or else…"

Kalyavan said, "Or …."

Before I spoke I moved my hand behind me and suddenly the soldiers were ready with their swords. I had sent a signal to Satyki.

“ Kalyavan, Friendship or your death…”

He laughed about hearing his death,

“… If you catch me, it will be my death.”

At that moment Satyki shouted and wild boars came running down the hill towards the soldiers and there was chaos all around. I took the opportunity and got lost in the forest. While running I realized kalyavan was behind me on his horse. For the next one day I tired him endlessly but I couldn’t think of a solution. Suddenly I saw a cave and a dog was coming out from that cave.

I decided to go inside it. There was still time for the three days to end. I climbed down from the tree and ran towards the cave and I could hear the horse behind me. There was light inside the cave and on the side was a man of the same built as mine meditating.

I realized it was Sage *Muchukund* and if anyone bothered his mediation his powers would burn that person to death. I covered him with my blanket and hid myself.

Tired due to lack of sleep Kalyavan was in rage and thinking it was me, started hitting the sage multiple times. The sage opened his eyes and in his anger burnt him. The burning fire, the sage's anger and the power of the chant killed Kalyavan in an instant, turning him into ash.

The sage's anger hadn't even calmed down when I came across him. I do not know what he saw or maybe he saw a glimpse of Vishnu in me. I blessed him and told him to calm his anger.

Maybe I could have tried to make Kalyavan understand and I could have united with him but from a political view it wouldn't have been right. Jarasandh's brain was inclined towards having a kingdom just like Kans. Kans had destroyed the republic of the Yadavs but he was our own and part of the Aryavarta. I did not want to leave Kalyavan alive because that would have sowed the seeds of tradition, a tradition where foreigners enter forcefully. These traditions get difficult to remove later.

By the time I left the cave, Satyki had ordered Kalyavan's army to leave. Now we had to look for our way back to our camp. But I think we were in a circle, because soon we were on the way to Gir and by night we were with Dau.

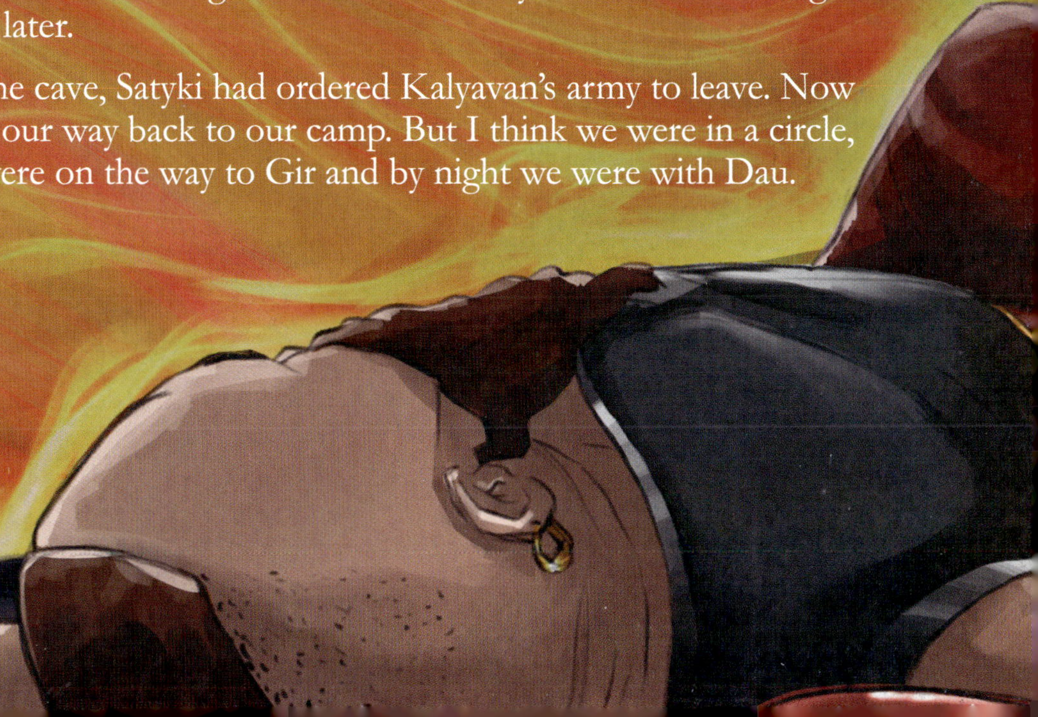

Memory is a weird thing, it diverts you. I have crossed this path multiple times, but today when I am crossing this path, after the war my memory board has a series of pictures and I remembered how I ran for the first time to save lives. And today I was tired, for the first time.

Sage Utang used to be lean in meditation but no sage or saint is away from politics. It wasn't selfish but the complete knowledge kept them invested in these incidents. My experience with Durvasa and the sages from the time of Rama, depict this. Utang too was caught with anger. The relation between Meditation and anger is still beyond me, maybe one of them is a lie. After welcoming me he asked me about the Pandav-Kaurav enmity and he said "Krishna, what you did was great, you stopped the war from happening." Maybe the news of the war hadn't reached him yet. That day was a day of weird experiences. The tiredness and now a sudden feeling of guilt. I lowered my eyes. "I couldn't stop the war."

The sage was a changed man now and he said "You couldn't stop it." He ate his words and said "Krishna."

I dared to not look up and said "I don't have the control over fate and time."

"You don't have control over time, and the world revolves around your actions". Utang was losing his calm but he controlled his anger and said "Where were you and Balram?"

"Balram was on pilgrimage and I was Arjuna's charioteer."

Every answer had a question, and one could see Utang getting angrier by the minute. "Krishna, you wanted the war to happen that is why you were there otherwise you could have left like Balaram, it wasn't your battle and by making the brothers fight you have destroyed everything." His anger was at its peak and he said "I will curse you for this sin."

For the first time after hearing Utang's words I felt a feeling coming to me from my subconscious mind. The guilt turned into fear. My brain was ready for defense, because sometime ago Gandhari's curse, the near end of my clan and now this. The doubt of the forbidden arose and a sudden ego for my powers. But at this age I was about to do something for the third time – to show my divine form, but I was doing this for myself, for the first time. I just used anger and hypnosis and said "I am time and I am the controller, you will curse me, Utang?!"

Everyone around us were scared because when I showed this form of mine at Duryodhana's court and in front of Arjuna before the war, I was calm but today I was enraged.

Sage Utang was shocked to see this side of me and he calmed down and folded his arms.

And then we did not say anything to each other and we left for Dwarka.

You must be thinking why am I narrating this. Utang did not curse me but I still remember his curious eyes "In the moment of trouble, Krishna, you too become a puppet in the hands of your feelings which arise at the time of death."

This incident left a little something else with me—My behavior, my fear of death which I had never known. This question still remains. That has nothing really changed. And the question that hasn't been solved since ages—what decides the fate of man—man's decision or time ? The scriptures, astrology, work everything is for the peace of mind and the satisfaction but the truth is far away. I knew the answer but without instigation I could not have found it. Everyone has to search for this answer, on their own.

Today when I look at the history of man, death is never simple, nor mine nor any other Krishna's. Whatever the name be, whatever temple he is caged in, everyone of them is a rebel. And then he may have helped with a pen or a sword, or might have said that the earth is not the center, the sun doesn't revolve around us or God is shapeless. All of them were in darkness, in fear, cutting the ropes of hatred, all through their lives.

I said the same things, I said praying to Lord Indra is a waste, worship who feeds you, who saves you. The crowd wasn't strong enough so I had to earn their belief by showing miracles. I had to hide them to protect them from rain in a cave in the mountains,and create an optical illusion which they mistook for me picking up the mountain. Some of them walked with me but most of them were scared. More than the struggle the easy way was to become God, not only me but also the Govardhan Mountain. They shut me in a temple and began to worship the mountain.

Sleeping people create gods with fear because they were helpless in front of the powers of both me and Rama otherwise and the people who tried to help them with intelligence or love were killed either by poison, sword, crucifix, bullet or by other violent ways.

I think looking at them, man realizes his weakness and tries to get over his inferiority. In the creation of God fear precedes love; true devotion is unconditional love.

The devotion out of fear and the god arising out of it has multiple layers. Every person asks for safety and comfort from the people above them and this paves the way for exploitation. Neither the king nor the politics let such instances go.In the moment of dire crisis and helplessness giving air to fear and then helping the people. At this time throwing them into war or making them a follower is easy. With time if the public is content, they start calling them god. Who doesn't like having an ego. Everything they do themselves, they spread the word about it, like a blessing is told to every scared human.

And once you have become a god, immortality and ego do not leave you.

The same risk was with me also. And seeing my popularity Pondrak had already declared himself Vasudeva. I had to erase him.

You can put the same blame on me. But I want to tell you, not in my defense, but from every Krishna, that we were never greedy for power and we have tried to free every human from slavery. We should learn the art of turning our resources into our strength and our belief in our decision. All we said was, don't make us into a god. Some understood us, some changed but the crowd was not brave enough to change themselves. If you don't believe me, read what was said by Socrates, Gandhi, Buddha and even me.

Between the King and his people, others also made their attempts at power– the brahmin's through knowledge, Vaishai's through money and they left the workers as outcasts and untouchables. They would have even made me untouchable if they were not scared of my powers. And in my words they did play this trick on me.

For hundreds of years they kept explaining *moksha* to the poor. *Dharam, Arth, Kaam* in other words material prosperity for the powerful and released from the misery of life, for the *Dalits*. *Dalits* were the ones who were suppressed. All they had was hollow knowledge, and how to endure the pain while keeping a calm mind. The search for happiness was a waste. But nobody left it themselves. Everything that could make life better was hidden and caught them in a web of troubles. The web of sins and good deeds was interwoven such that man died trying to un-mesh it. Nobody said anything about how this sin-virtue was not set in stone and not everyone had to walk on it. Every human has to make their own balance, their own limits. For what they had to be alert was *aasakti* (addiction) because that is truly a shackle.

But in the hopelessness of one is the power of the other. I spread happiness to the common man but after me the powerful did not like it, especially the Brahmins because they had controlled Rama but neither Vyas nor I gave them importance. I was apprehensive that they would use me for their profit, at my expense. But if you want to meet me leave the knowledge of the Brahmins and come near my heart.

The Gita that this land has kept so close to their heart, it's time you hear it again. Like I had to present my divine form thrice, just like that the moral of life had to be explained multiple times to multiple people. Whatever I said was to control the situation at least in the case of Arjuna. I had said it to Udhav to give him a message.

I was a man of doing, not a man of analyzing work. To comment on fate and it's stories was not my job. So that is why I tried to tell the gist of life through my experiences.

But people made it the Gita and looking at today's Gita I am beginning to doubt my own words. Every person has added their own arguments . There are less questions, more answers.

Now, even I will turn every conversation as Gita and talk about the situation and will leave the use of it on you. Sometimes you even have to act the Gita out. I had to live the entire Gita.

I had a friend, Sudama, simple, fearful but full of love for me. I got busy with Dwarka and he was left behind in Mathura. I had forgotten to check up on him. One day the guards informed me of a poor beggar standing at the gate and calling himself my friend. I came out and found Sudama.

He was standing there in his torn clothes and weak body.I hugged him within seconds and brought him inside. He wasn't sure if I would recognize him. I made him sit on the chair and showed him my love. I was washing his feet and my tears were mixing with the water. Everyone was looking at us, shell shocked till I did not tell them the story of our childhood. Sudama's wife had reminded him of our friendship and had sent him here by saying that one friend was God and the other was poor. Sudama could not ask for anything but to avoid fighting with his wife, he travelled to Dwaraka, facing multiple obstacles. While eating I realized he was hiding something. I snatched the sack from him, it had rice, for me as a gift but he was hesitating because of the difference between us.

It wasn't limited to me now. On one hand it was my trust and love and on the other it was the public's problems' horrid face. The difference between poor and rich that gives rise to hesitation. It didn't take me time to establish love. There was no shortage in Sudama's hospitality. Rukmani had also considered him like a brother. Every time he tried to leave, I used to stop him. After a few months he was too eager to go. I said my farewell and gave him a chariot and some guards. When he was leaving his mental state was not unknown to me. He was sent for help and he got lost in love. He couldn't say it and now both poverty and his wife had to be faced, empty handed. But like I said I could not sit idle and I had to follow my Dharma. I had to fix the problem as well and not just analyze it. My people took him to a place near Dwaraka, near the sea shore, that was freshly constructed. His wife had been called. I was told later that Sudama could not believe it but his wife was really happy because she was now the head of Sudamapuri. He had this right over my prosperity. It was an opportunity for me to live my own Gita by rising above the self.

My brother, Udhav, wanted a message from me when I was leaving this earth. *Udhav Gita* was the framework born from my tries at life, the balance of life. But just as I had thought people had forgotten it, what they remembered was what I had told Arjuna, before the war. Making me God made my words important too—called it the Bhagavata Gita.

I smile even today when I think of that day.

It had been a few years since Draupadi was shamed in the Kaurava court. The exile of the Pandavas and the peace deal had also failed. Kurukshetra was prepared for war. Besides the warriors, the helpers, the cleaners, doctors, funeral helpers were all gathered in this place, that place that I had named Dharamshetra.

The kings of Aryavart had chosen their sides according to friendship and relations. Everyone knew everyone's strengths. The rules were set, but no one knew who would leave this place alive. Everyone was holding their Dharma right.

That night when I was passing through the camps I was engulfed by a sense of shock. The one person I wanted to meet that night was Shakuni. But because of the fear of people I could not. Whatever it was, his mind was divided because both the sides were one family. And what could I have done, I was divided too.

I was far away from Hastinapur, in Dwarka and was waiting for time to play it's next dice. But what could I do about the bad habits of time? That day while discussing Dwarka's future with Dau I slept and when I woke up Dau had left. Habitually his love for me could not let him see me in pain. Even if I was wrong.

That day my mind was working even when I was sleeping. I suddenly woke up and I saw someone standing there. Who could the guard let in before I was up. It was cleared when I saw Arjuna. Even before I could get up and hug Arjuna I heard a voice from behind me, "Vasudev, I am here too".

I knew this voice, even in politeness one could feel the existence.

It was Duryodhana. He was as knowledgeable as Yudhishthira, as powerful as Bheem but his nurture and nature was stuck on his self-dharma.

Forgetting Arjuna and keeping in mind the traditions of the world I hugged Duryodhana first and then Arjuna. Nobody would have believed that a few days back Duryodhana wanted to capture and enslave me and Satyki had to take his weapons out to protect me. He had readied the chariot and on my one signal he would have ended the Kauravas. My army in order to protect me would have finished everyth ing there was of the Kauravas. But this was not my struggle and to protect myself creating such havoc would be selfishness.

Little anger, some loud voice tone and some hypnosis was enough to spread fright, and me on the chariot - vanishing. Me and my friends knew this art of defeating enemies with trickery since we were kids. This must have been enough for someone to know me and to stay far from me but not Duryodhana, this was why he was not Suyodhana, he was Duryodhana.

My anger had an opposite effect on him, I was about to know this in a short while.

"Two great men together; here. I am blessed", I said.

Both of them said in sync, "we need your help".

"What happened that both of you need my help?

I hope it's not for the same thing."

I knew what they wanted but I wanted to lighten the mood. So I used sarcasm in my tone because two men who were enemies, could shoot poisonous words at each other any moment. Both of them disliked my light tone.

Duryodhana said "Madhav, the war is inevitable now".

I thought he was telling me even though I had just told him the same thing!

Arjuna was standing with folded arms.

"And you, Parth. What is your problem..? I was trying to be ignorant.

I did not want to get stuck in anything by saying things myself. Especially to these great warriors.

Arjuna said "We both need your help, in the war."

"You tell me what you want, let Duryodhana speak for himself."

Duryodhana said "I am older and I came to your room before Arjuna, that is why I have the right to ask first."

"But I saw Arjuna first." I said this and turned towards both of them and suggested, "This is not my war, and I will not take the blame for the destruction it will cause."

Even if I went or not, the ownership for this calamity was to fall on my head and the only one to share this was Shakuni. Everyone else would explain their sides, keeping history as witness.

Both of them spoke together again, "Your presence will keep everything in control."

Two contradictions uttered the same sentence, both the sides broke their limits, nothing was less or more, both of them disagreed with me and now. I was around people who after the cloth is torn, they want to sew it. But I had already thought of an answer and presented them with my decision.

"Fine. I will be present, but I will not pick up arms."

This was a boon for Duryodhana and I could see a gleam of happiness on his face- "So you will only come for justice?"

"You brothers have made justice impossible for me, now I will only be a witness. (I had spoken Gita's first sentence that day). But I cannot stay idle, I will be a charioteer."

I wanted to see the reaction from both of them. Arjuna was disappointed and Duryodhana was happy.

I continued "If I stay away from the war of the *Aryavart* and if I stay neutral I will be cursed. That is why I am giving you a chance to choose-- Me as a charioteer on one side and on the other side my entire *Narayani* Army with their entire power and I promise they will fight against me."

In their influence even I had begun talking in orders. The follower of visible power, Duryodhana, did not waste even a second and asked for my army. Arjuna was happy to have me. My worry was not the war but it was for the storm that was heading my way. Both of them bid me farewell and went to meet Dau and I was waiting for his anger to burst.

Dau was in the mind that I should stay away from this war and that I was biased towards the Pandavas, and his anger was justified as Duryodhana was his student. Dau was angry and right before the war started he gave me his love and left on a pilgrimage on the trail of *Saraswati,* where the war was about to begin.

And now, right at the beginning of the war, when all hearts were beating and all nerves were fluttering, the conches had been blown, the armies were ready and Arjuna had told me to take the chariot right in the center of both the armies. I was shocked but I was the charioteer. I brought and halted the chariot at a point. After some time Arjuna sat down and said "I will not fight."

For a moment the land beneath my feet shook, everything was falling apart. Arjuna was not only a warrior, he was also my reflection, my arrow to establish *dharma*. The war would have happened without Arjuna as well but nothing would have been successful. For once I thought of leaving being a charioteer behind and started ordering him instead. He would have fought, but with half his heart, and when I saw his condition, sweating and scared of looking at death, I started thinking.

To divert his mind I said something to him and he kept asking me questions. He kept asking me questions and I kept answering them and a subtle train of thought was born, that later became the Gita. I had said all that to Arjuna that day, there was nobody else around us, but how these thoughts reached the people, is still a mystery, that was solved after a very long time.

After the war was over and I was leaving, Arjuna said- "Madhav, I have a request."

"What?"

"That day before the war started, you had cleared my doubts, my wish is that you tell them to me once again."

"Arjuna, you are a treasure of good will, you can defeat sleep with your calm mind, did you ask those questions unconsciously ?"

"No, Madhav. I was awake and whatever you told me I have tried to apply to my life as well. But something I still haven't understood. If you repeat them I will understand."

Arjuna's answer did not convince me and the reason for repeating the Gita became the *Anu-Gita*. But that is when I came to know how these things reached others.

Arjuna, everyday kept repeating the things he remembered and kept telling them to some of his army. This kept spreading and even reached the writer of Krishna's divinity, Vyas. Wherever there was a gap in knowledge, the heart of the poet filled it.

But once words have been spoken, they are not the speaker's alone.

Whatever I had explained was in accordance with the situation, when a warrior was going against his religion. The man who talked about wit and wisdom was acting like a scared goat.

What later became the words of God, was actually a psychological treatment, of a person stuck in doubt. He had to be shown the way, every way possible.

Human's mind is made this way, duality and hopelessness is present in every living second, a child is free of this but he is taught this through wrong and right, putting

the child in the same framework. Some grow up on their own will but mostly grow up with the same framework,Why ?

Because the ropes of duality are hard to walk on, every second there is a fear of falling.

There is death on every step, that gives birth to new ones and forgets the old . Some day the first is forgotten and the new doesn't arrive, this is the moment the human mind is scared of, the end of life in a single moment, this fills in the mind a meaninglessness. The common man lives with this and they focus so much on the fear that they give rise to power. Some feel confident walking on such paths till they don't face someone or something against them. That day even I learnt something-- Arjuna who I thought was above duality was actually stuck in a dispute, because of the fear of death, his own or others. That

day I realised this duality will never end, will only be hidden, in the folds of the brain and with the first opportunity this duality will come out

because of fear.

And that is because man, his memory or in his future, living in the moment and staying free from the directions of time is actually the freedom from death. But the mind has to be kept busy, because in that moment time becomes an arrow and turns into a circle.The past and the future is all visible. But this can only be done by Shiva. To become Shiva one has to be vigilant all the time or else an animal's urges can take its claws out at any time.

The answer to this contradiction is what you call the Gita.

Gita is just this, anyone who reads it today, my only advice is to learn the ways to follow the path that matches their nature.

Times change, goals change and that is why the routes change too. To walk with time what is important is to choose the right path, the right nature and nurture and balance them. The art of finding is necessary. It is shocking to see that sages and the people on death beds read this, Gita should be told to the children and the youth, because they will change the society. The Gita is of the future, not the past.

I had warned while delivering the *Anu-Gita*, I am not sure if Arjuna actually understood it, I am not sure if you will get it or not. Vedas, Puranas, dharmashastras, even the Gita are all set in the same place. Some of them are the truths of life and some are path changing orders. Not everything is for everyone, new visions are important and so are new authors. Dharma will keep changing and so will the behaviours. But till the mind remains like this, every human will have to search for these truths, for themselves and the society. Maybe my thoughts help, but these are not written in stone, these are just guiding lights which are like a lighthouse for the ships at sea.

What had I said ?

That day I wanted to tell Arjuna "To get up, and fight." But a mind in doubt feels trapped. That is why I had said-

"You need to fulfill your duties and follow the societal duties, not for yourself but by sacrificing yourself, with a selfless thought and while doing so, focus on the work and not on the results."

Was it difficult to understand and do ? It was difficult for Arjuna too and instead of shooting arrows he started shooting questions at me. Later I thought, if I had said this in easy words, I would have saved time.

In reality, what I wanted to say was, "wise words and foolish actions. Arjuna, all your life you carried your *Gandiva* with you, collected arms, to become the greatest archer. The small battles were a waste if at the time like this you are acting like a sage."

This is what you called the Gita.

But Arjuna's questions had made it necessary for me to show him the paths -- of knowledge, yoga, belief and work, Self and the other, heaven and earth, the reality of life and the myth of life- but all of this was not just my divinity, it was the way of my life. That was the first time I had made it a vision of my life.

It was just one thing; life and death, the whole universe, the past, the future, everything that is dear to man,everything was tied by a

thread of God.

I had to become God to convince him.

"Shloka"(34)

"Mamekam Sharanam" --- Come to me and drop all that you know.

I had to show this side to Arjuna. I had to show my divine form. Everything that was life, was in me. That day it was necessary to end duality, because war was inevitable. Otherwise, humans can find God whenever they are in trouble.

After this Arjuna was free and I turned the chariot towards the battle ground.

Was I teaching violence ? No; I was just reminding about duty, the balance between the mind and the brain without getting attached. Violence was the choice made by the Pandavas and the Kauravas, and when they had chosen it, what was the point of doubt.

Not only Uttang, a lot of people want to ask me this, that if I had the power why did I not stop the war. I had tried but later I thought that my subconscious mind wanted the opposite. In the open, peace and in the hidden; war. Is it not true for most of us, still?

I had promised someone, the end of evil.

Stopping at this story and changing the mood, I will have to go back a long time, both in age and place.

From Vrindavan and my life, from my childhood to my youth.

I had as many *sakhiyan's* and *sakhas*. The sakhas were my age, but the female sakhiyan were both younger or older to me, but the one who stayed as my love was the woman you know as *Radha*. When I left for Mathura on Kansa Uncle's call there was chaos all over. I had thought I would return, so I did not pay much attention to it.

They called me heartless and so much more. Whenever I treat prosperity, power, influence or love as a hermit, people begin to see me as emotionless.

That day my beloved Radha, who was my life, was silent, she didn't even cry and she let me go. After a long time I realised that Radha had set me free from the human form of love, she had let me go so that I could become universal love. I will talk about Radha later, I don't wish to mix her story now, right now I want to tell you the reason for the war.

After defeating Kansa at Mathura and after crowning my maternal grandfather Ugrasen as the king, I freed my parents and before I could take a breath I was pulled into the politics of the Aryavarta. Kansa wanted to kill me because he was believing a prophecy that the eight child of *Devaki* would be the reason for his death. I don't know if I would have been that but he did what everyone else does, he made this goal his life because of fear. He captured *Vasudeva* and Devaki and he had killed my 7 brothers and sisters. It became necessary to protect me so as soon as I was born I was taken to Gokul, to *Nand Baba* and *Yashoda maa*.

After many years had passed with a wish to kill Dau and

me, he had called us to Mathura. It was stupid, because even after I was born, he had ruled for 16 years. But the greed for immortality!

His death was not our plan. At that time both me and Dau were ignorant about politics and were inside a prison. That time when Mathura was overwhelmed, grateful and happily in love with Dau and me, I became an adult without my will. I could see a death storm emerging behind the happiness of the people. We did not know Kansa's father in law was the king of Magadha, the great warrior Jarasandh. Jarasandh started attacking Mathura after he heard of Kansa's death and my life moved from love in Vrindavan, to fighting battles. My days of play were stopped, abruptly.From that moment only, I got used to removing my mind from the things around me and to start looking beyond it, I could see the arriving future. You just need skills for this, you don't have to become a God.

However, I was not bereft of love.

The paths of my life at times felt like I was paying off debts. I was freeing the women by cutting down their shackles. Whether it was raasa at Vrindavan or the love of Radha, or the relations I was yet to make, were the stories of me saving enslaved women. Every woman who rebelled and who tried to change their life, found Krishna, standing outside the house, ready to help. If they don't step out, then there is not much that even I could do, then and even now.

The societal pressure that had stopped Rama from freeing women did not bother me much for I was out to set new rules and trying to find new ways had become a part of my life.

But after Radha, where love blossomed under the impact of death, I would not have anything personal left for me, it was all a struggle between love and politics.

Giving a name to every relation was not possible, after all who was Shabri for Ram ?

As soon as I entered Mathura, she met me, violated, rude and disfigured, Kubja. I became curious to know the reason for her pitiful situation because I saw what was hidden. The beauty of her past and her eyes had the glimmer of years of patience and hope.

"After all you came ?"

Even in the danger of death looming around us, I could not ignore her, I sent Dau and I left with her.

After a few hours when I left her house, Kubja had changed.

Whatever she said that day, maybe, was the Gita. The incomplete Kubja was now complete because I had said that what was important was me and her. I had said that to her to give confidence, to give her happiness, but she had changed. That day I realised the power of my words, till now my friends used to believe my stories, but this time I believed them myself. From that day I use my words only when I know the impact. I have heard that from the next day, the people of Mathura had begun to find her beautiful. The way of looking at things changed, the creation changed.

Bearing the attacks of Jarasandh, Mathura was a wreck. Dau and I, far away from Jarasandh, on the West coast made Dwarka and reached there. On the large sea shore, we were given land by the tribes who were living there because we hadn't challenged their existence but instead opened ways to protect them. In my view the impact was from the time when Dau and me had rescued Guru Sandipini's son from Shankasur to pay our Guru Dakshina. My conch had the sound like that of the thunder of the sea, my conch Panchjanya, never left my side.

But we were not free from Jarasandh. Because of the pressure, we had to jump into politics again. With new friends, we made new enemies as well.

Rukmini's brother, Rukmi had fixed her marriage with Shishupal. This relation was with Jarasandh as a friend but Shishupal was my brother. My problem was solved when Rukmini told me that she would marry only me or else she would kill herself. I was a bit doubtful but Dau had made up his mind. To ignore Rukmini's words would not only have been her disrespect but also a danger. My doubt was about how to rescue her from the palace. Rukmini herself solved this problem for me. While she prayed at the temple, I would kidnap her. Everything happened, I got married to Rukmini, and as gifts I had 4 new enemies.

Seven new wives, everyone of them in a different trouble, all of them free, brave and could take their decisions. The only woman who could live with me was a woman who was independent. Satyabhama was a warrior, Jambwanti was strong but Rukmini was balanced. After Radha, Rukmini had freed me from all household duties and that is the reason why I could manage establishing dharma in the world. Satyabhama took me to the east, Praagjyotish till the place of desire where Narkasur had captured 16 thousand women and was torturing them. Having had the boon of immortality Narkasur was a formidable enemy.

It was after a fierce war that I could free these women. I did not know that I had invited more trouble for me. As if I didn't already have enough duties.

When I freed these women, and told them to go home, they denied it.

I got the first shock when they told me the reason, after living at a man's place nobody would accept them, neither their husbands nor their sons. A woman's respect and her insult in a male dominated world is not in their own hands. All of a sudden I remembered Rama when he sacrificed Sita, on a single person's sarcastic comment.

Krishna could not let this happen. I had only one thought in my mind, how to reestablish these women in the society. After thinking for a while, I talked to the women and called the Yadava warriors.

I asked every warrior to marry 2 or 3 of these women (it was normal those days) so that we could take them to Dwarka and give them societal respect. All of them said in unison- "No, Vasudeva, We cannot do this. We can't keep our own wives happy, 2- 3 will turn into a civil war."

Now I had to solve this problem. Satyabhama's knowledge and large heartedness came to help, she gave me a suggestion and I said - "From today all these women are Krishna's wives, if they don't have a problem.Take them to Dwarka and establish a new town. They will get the same respect as my wives."

I presented women liberation in one instance and one more exodus started, this time from East to West. But I knew that in the future this question would arise for all these women. Why did I make them my wives, why not sisters or daughters ?

Because the relations of sister or daughter are an instinctive relation determined by birth, that which is not born, friendship, could still be made. The feeling that I have lived with is the feeling of friendship. I could have kept these women in Dwarka just like that, nobody could have said anything out of fear, but in the future I would have been a bad example or labelled as a question on my character but few thought like this. Most called this as my play or leela.

By becoming a wife they got their societal respect back. This was the rule of my times that one had to marry. But it was not necessary for a man and woman to have hierarchy, the husband was not the master of his wife, this was the making of the future.

I had broken this ritual in love, Radha was married and both of us never thought of that, we just wanted to show the world that marriage is not needed for love. But people don't have that courage.

These 16 thousand women were different, neither was I in that position where I could have revolted for love nor was it required. My mind was stuck in the forthcoming war and by making them my sisters or calling them my daughters, I would have to fulfill the responsibilities like those of remarriage etc. All of them were of different ages and had been violated by Narkasur-- both physically and mentally, the problem would have remained the same -- Who would accept them?

I had asked them and they had cried about the same thing. There was no other way to solve their problems in one go. If I would have kept them without making them my wife, they would have become the object of desire for the men. They were safe because they were Krishna's wives, under Satybhama's care and they were free. I told you, I don't talk. I work. You can narrate.

Once I reached Dwarka, I had no time to meet them and they never desired it. I used to get to hear about them, from Satyabhama. But even today it is counted that I have 16 thousand and eight wives, but I am called after the love that I had lost -- Radha Krishna.

Me who was neither in leaving nor in holding, in denial or in acceptance --This was one relation that I could not leave nor keep. There I was the same in colour - Black, the meaning of Krishna. There are three dark Krishnas- Me, Vyas and Krishnaa.

Draupadi or Krishnaa whose love was complete even without having my love. There was a need for a man who could face Draupadi's wit and shine and at that time and I was quite popular in Aryavart. Maybe Draupadi would have married me and I would have accepted. But when Drupad told me about the motive of her life I explained it to Krishnaa. I didn't sleep that night, because what was mine, in following my duties I left it, yet again. But this time I gave it a new shape, a new relation- the Sakha. I could not fully give myself to this relation and I kept running. The eye of the fish was not the target, Arjuna's arrow had hit me.

Krishnaa used to say that I fulfilled my promise, whenever she needed me, I was there. But I always show my love by hurting. I kept taking all her problems like a cloud to the extent that I saw her marry my brothers, saw her marrying five instead of 'The one'.

That day when Arjuna ,dressed like a Brahmin shot the eye of the fish, I had recognised the Pandavas. I had already told her that in the entire Aryavart there was none other than Arjuna and Karna who could pass the test. Now she had to decide and with her my silent conversations were enough. She called Karna a charioteer's son and sparked a fire of hatred.

I was still in the mini-battle that had erupted between kings and the other Pandavas. Like all fathers Druapd too wanted to send his daughter off with grandeur. But in a situation like this I did not want to disclose the identity of the Pandavas and told Druapd that till she stayed there the other kings would create too much trouble. Even he couldn't recognise the Pandavas. I let Draupadi go and consoled Drupad and told him that I would go and check.

Feelings in the heart create doubts in the mind, and I was witnessing that. Drupad had doubts about anyone hitting the fish's eye, in the magic and in the search for a son in law, he forgot to ask about Arjuna's family. In times like these my brain used to be alert, feelings hardly overpowered me. Draupadi was mine and she was going to be someone else's, I was worried not angry. Maybe this was the reason why my behaviour was different

from others. In people's eyes, I was God but the truth was the same, do what is right, and not to worry about the results.

As soon as Draupadi left, me and Dau started walking behind them, towards their forest abode. More than meeting the Pandavas, I was worried about Draupadi. And I was doubtful, because of what I had heard, I was scared and that is exactly what happened. Even before I reached, Kunti had, without seeing, told her sons to divide whatever they had got, just like always. She did show remorse and guilt but I was not ready to believe her. She must have thought that Arjuna was in the middle and because of a beautiful woman the elders and the younger ones could get jealous. She knew her sons. This was beyond my acceptance but I was helpless, I had pushed her into this fire. That moment I had pledged to live with Draupadi like a shadow. Not physically but with the power of the mind.

For this reason alone I did not end the spread of misconceptions about my character and instead blessed Kunti and the Pandavas. I was younger to them but it was important to establish the aura of the God around me.

Actually, Draupadi had invited this trouble herself, she had a fire burning but she could not use it to her potential. She kept asking Shiva for particular traits in her husband, which were impossible to establish in one brain and body, other than me, so Shiva got frustrated and agreed,she got all that she wished in the husbands but got split in five bodies.And left me to re-establish honour.

And this did happen multiple times, when I had to travel mentally. I heard Draupadi's calling every time even if I was stuck in a problem.

I used to reach Hastinapur from Dwarka on every tear that Draupadi shed. To save her from Durvasa's anger and her sadness I had to face a challenge that almost exhausted my mental powers, that may be called telepathy today. Durvasa had asked Draupadi for food for him and his fellow sages, but she had no food at home. At that time I was with Rukmini and I started feeling anxious. Rukmini knew about this.

I meditated and reached near Draupadi, She told Durvasa to go and bathe and she got some time to communicate with me.I used the same mental power to satiate the sage's hunger. Durvasa had the power to see beyond the hidden, he knew this was my doing.

He never forgot that. Like I said nothing happens without a reason.

After ages, Durvasa reached Dwarka and directly entered my sleeping chambers. Looking at him I realized that if anything goes wrong today, I will be cursed. I told Rukmini to follow all his orders and both of us started

taking care of him. After eating he asked for kheer and then told us to remove all our clothes, Rukmini was shocked, but I signalled her to do so. Then Durvasa told us to apply the Kheer on our bodies. Rukmini was in shock but she continued doing it because of the fear of being cursed.

Durvasa then asked us to go around Dwarka on a chariot. As soon as he sat on the chariot he let go of the horses and told Rukmini and me to pull the chariot. He hit only me with the whip as if testing me. Dwarka had closed its eyes. After a while when his anger settled down, he blessed us and he said to me "Where ever you have been hit by me, Krishna, no weapon of this world can harm you if it hits there."

The soles of my feet remained unmarked by Durvasa's whip; it must have a hidden message. It was for Jara.

But Draupadi's pain was beyond my endurance; the cost of it was heavy.

If it was possible I would have first punished her husbands for their weakness, for playing dice for greed and for pledging something and not having the power to complete it.

And then the Kauravas.

But if I could separate Draupadi from me because of my duty, and keep her away from the most eligible man after me, Karna whom I could stop by getting Draupadi to insult him, then that same duty could be protected by me. And maybe I could have found a solution for the torture inflicted on the Pandavas.

But the two mistakes had closed all doors of my mind. Yudhisthira's waging Draupadi in the game of dice and the disrobement of Krishnaa in the Kaurava court. Now this age had to finish for it had crossed the limit of Adharma, this was the first thought I had. For once I wanted to punish everyone in that court but I didn't want to overstep my rights. They had to fight themselves, whoever won would be less evil.

When I was taking a peace offering to Hastinapur, Krishnaa reminded me that once in a crowded court, she had torn her sari to stop the blood from my bleeding hand.

I remembered that after enduring Shishupal's abuses, I had taken out my Sudarshan Chakra. During the Rajasuya yagna when the Pandavas had honoured me, his jealousy had turned venomous. He insulted Bhishma and the Pandavas but he only wanted to abuse me. As soon his attention fell on me, the anger and revenge that he had bottled for years burst open. He kept shouting ,disinhibited and indecent. As soon as 100 abuses were said, my finger started moving. I had many ways to defeat him but I did not want to create a scene, either way Sudarshan was on my finger by then.Maybe I was looking rather angry, cause Bhishma was standing with his hands folded. I had promised his mother that I would listen to his 100 abuses. In one second his head was on the ground.In the process of killing him, I hurt myself and started bleeding and forgetting all her concerns, Draupadi tore her saree and tied it on my finger. I whispered to her, "I hope this love doesn't annoy your husbands." Draupadi smiled. I later thought that if I could hear 100 abuses, then I could have heard 200 too. But the question wasn't about my endurance, it was about Shishupal's limit and that had been decided. I was only doing my job.

Krishnaa said "You promised to avenge me, every sinner will bleed and now you are taking a peace deal. You repaid me for the sari by covering me with a cloth that day, but you still have to pay me back for the blood. This repayment cannot happen without blood."

"Krishnaa, for one revenge you cannot punish the entire kingdom."

I added- "And your revenge will be taken, trust me."

Draupadi was angry and she kept mumbling something, I don't remember. The ones you love, you don't remember their anger. She had apologised to me later.

At that moment I held Draupadi and let her anger flow.

My mind was stuck more on the Kaurava court than on Draupadi. What will happen if Duryodhana accepts the proposal ? But I was sure of one person- Shakuni.

I knew he would not let the war get delayed.

I left no stone unturned in the Kaurava court, I talked about the ignorance of the elders, Karna's shaming and the cowardness of the warriors. Then I asked for 5 villages. If Duryodhana had agreed to this his political sense would have fallen in my eyes. The five villages I had asked for were near the Yamuna bank. These were -Indraprastha (Delhi), Swarnaprastha(Sonipat), Panprastha (Panipat), Vyaghraprastha(Bagpat) and Tilprastha (Tilpat). The Pandavas would have had the West of the Yamuna and the east of the Ganga would have their supporters. Hastinapur couldn't have been moved.

Duryodhana would have been blamed for rejecting the proposal and starting a war. But he was right for rejecting it and for being angry at me because the Pandavas weren't this smart. And I have already told you what I did. The thought in my head was "Krishnaa, the war has begun."

The Vedas talk about the importance of sentences, like words have their own world. Amongst the many names that I have, one is 'Chhaliya'. The people who loved me took it differently but the 'chhal' in the name was completely different during the war., it was deceit. If someone else would have done this I would have called them the same thing. Even today when someone writes my story or talks about it, it stays within the boundary of love and they cannot accept the 'chhal' and they just ignore it as my miracles.

My definition of love was not limited and for me love was not limited to money that would get exhausted one day. Every love is complete and dividing each other is out of the question. My wives because of this reason, tried Draupadi and Radha's love, it was useless, but I let them do it, because I had understood, it was useless to compare two different things. That was personal but war was political.

There was a personal reason for all of this. I knew what had happened with Rama and how his religion, duty, society had held him and his beloved, Sita had to give her character certificate continuously. I had a loan to repay, Rama's and of every woman who could not get justice. I had come to free them, to break every shackle. I did break them, I broke every vision. But I had to leave Radha and as soon as I felt her loss, I understood that the world will also make me Rama. That moment I left my flute and picked up my Sudarshana Chakra and pledged to never sacrifice love again.

I was not doubtful about the strength of the Pandavas but I was doubtful about their wit. To manage five brothers, to keep them united and to remind them of their duty, first Kunti and then Draupadi were needed. For an unmanageable problem, I was there. They couldn't have gotten their kingdom if Draupadi had not reminded them, maybe living and being born in exile ,running was in their blood. But it was in Kunti's blood, not in Krishnaa's.

Both of them could not fight in the war. There is a battleground beyond the war zone that is of diplomacy. Wars are fought to be won, and it was imperative that the Pandavas won.Out of the people then, they were the only few humans. I was a charioteer but I knew the politics of the Aryavart. If I wanted I could have stayed in Dwarka but my motive to come on this earth would have not been fulfilled. Every person is born or dies because of a reason, call it destiny but efforts were the freedom to choose the way. This is why the three gunas - truth, darkness and desire are present in all of us in different quantities. After being born their surroundings, nourishment and challenges let them shine. We can always change our personality trait by practicing.With the blessing of God, I was born with all three equally and the conditions of life never let the darkness prevail.

The war that is talked about in Jaya by Vyas, is said to be written by Ganesha himself, on the condition that he wouldn't stop while writing, on which Vyas had asked him to pledge that he won't write without understanding. Now in the middle, someone as learned as Vyas also needed a moment to maintain the flow, he needed breaks, so in between he would narrate an unrelated story, till the time Ganesha understood the story, Vyas could regain his thoughts and make a story. He had told me this secret and I had insisted that in the future people might take this for granted and might add their own stories. I have heard his 24, 000 versed story is now at a lakh verses. And this caused me the maximum loss. Vyas had kept my story limited but the new writers made me divine.

The same had happened with Rama, his story was told by Sita, but what was not known was made up by Valmiki. Valmiki's knowledge was not imaginative, it was true knowledge. He was a bandit in the forests of middle India, whatever he got he used to steal but what he wrote became history and without knowing the geography, nobody could write this. From the bridge between Lanka and India to the powers of the monkey army, from the flowers to the soil, he knew everything. It can be said that the businessmen who came from the South, Valmiki used to kill them after he received all their knowledge. He weaved it such in the story of Rama that the jumps of imagination could do no harm. Destiny didn't have this grace on me.

You saw how difficult my life was and then people added more troubles to it. There is no doubt that the story of the battle was made into an epic by these imaginative poets by adding Dharma, duty, right and wrong to it through the medium of stories. And this is not all, they joined it such that all of this feels like an epic, except my life, which made my life divine because by the time this was written I was already a part of folk tales and the eight avatar as well.

I kept working and the stories kept getting weaved around me, from one mouth to the other with new miracles being added.

I hadn't said "war has begun " to Draupadi alone, my war had started way before the Kuru war. I had challenged the power of Indra, the killers of Kansa, both me and my brothers used to defeat them but there are some incidents that not only change your position but also follow you all through your life. Like Jarasandh, who I had defeated only before the Mahabharata war. If one sees it deeply no incident leaves us, the Indra I had defeated, his son Arjuna was my most loved. But there was something bigger than this.

During my childhood while playing near the river I had done a brave thing.On the banks of Yamuna lived some tribes and they kept the river in their control.There used to be internal struggles within the tribes. We cow herds weren't looking for our ownership of the water nor were we bothered about the use of that river's waters. Among these the Naga were the strongest, one part of the Yamuna was under them and the pirates were their soldiers. Someone had learnt the art of capturing a snake and they kept scaring everyone, either as a snake or in a disguised form. A major part of Yamuna's water was an important part of our life. But no cow herd or woman could go far for water, who ever went far either did not return or was injured. A small water bank had

been left safe for us. The snake-humans were a little different from us in their animal tendencies.

That day I took my friends and went a little far and while playing I tossed the ball into the river. I had thrown it on purpose, I wanted to see the land of the snakes, and I jumped into the river to get the ball. As I was going deeper I could hear my friends on the shore shouting "Dau save Kanha, he has jumped into the river." I was careful but scared, I knew Dau would not have come after me. He himself had said that Yamuna had to be freed.

As soon as I reached the depth of the river I heard a voice and an angry snake was coming towards me. I raised myself a bit and I saw it was a human because the length and height was not of a snake. I knew it was Kaaliya. In an instance a fight started under the water and the tides began to rise and the voices from the shore also increased. I think everyone was thinking that Kaaliya had bitten me. I was fighting less but saving myself from the tides. I had more practice of holding my breath underwater than Kaaliya, sometimes when my head appeared above the water the people on the shore shouted louder. For a moment, on Kaaliya's neck, pushing him into the water, I came up and saw Dau. His eyes asked me if I would be able to handle it or should he come, my eyes asked for his permission to finish Kaaliya. Dau raised his hand and put his thumb down, now Kaaliya would die. As soon as I put pressure on the throat Kaaliya got scared and asked for forgiveness, helpless moments kill all egos. I said "From today your rule is over, I will reveal your truth, your dead body will clear all fears." Kaaliya pleaded "Krishna, I will leave, all of this was to survive. If we wouldn't have scared people, Kansa's men would have made us leave, even we have a right to live."

I said- "Living by scaring people is cowardice, but I am letting you go. I have to end the fear before you leave or humans will begin to hate snakes. Tell me how to do this."

Then Kaaliya, in his snake form spread his head like a fan and he made me stand on it and raised his head above the water, while hiding his human face.I stood in one position, like a winner, calm and holding the flute to my lips.This game of mine has now become a statue and an idol. But I was worried because of something else.

If work was pitiless then time was strong and I didn't believe in destiny. Few years later when I had to make Indraprastha for the Pandavas, Me, who had left Kaaliya for life, had burned Khandavprastha. There were a lot of Nagas that lived there but they were with the Kauravas. I didn't even think about how many died and how many survived. They must have also forgotten my kind behaviour towards Kaaliya. My mistake was that this enmity kept going on till the time of Janamjeya, Arjuna's Great-grandson, and this was when the Mahabharata was narrated.

All of this was not a great problem, but you didn't notice, when I was defeating Kaaliya, I was not at all scared because with Dau around I never am.

Later who made me into an avatar called Balaram an avatar of Sheshnag. Why not ? I, Vishnu was carrying the burdens of the world, and since I stepped on the Earth Sheshnaag was carrying me as was Dau carrying me . But Dau never reprimanded me for my acts towards the nagas.

But my love for the Pandavas made him angry, he thought except Bheem all the brothers were lost. Neither could they make a decision nor fight for their rights on their own. He believed that in a family feud we should be neutral. The fuel to this fire was when Arjuna took Subhadra from Dwarka. Dau got angry and started going after Arjuna with arms. If Dau had caught Arjuna that day, nobody would have been able to save him, not even Yamraj. That day it was very difficult for me to stop him, I even had to say that Subhadra was my sister as well, I would not want anything bad for her. Dau left after this but his feelings for the Pandavas got worse.

Maybe, Dau was not wrong and so was his staying neutral but I didn't have the power to do this because I couldn't have left the path of righteousness and duty. I also took a breath because I could have seen the war like a catastrophe from a chariot, but Balram couldn't. If he had been there, he would have fought and the side he favoured would have won, I knew it was the Kauravas. I had fought with Shiva once, but I could not fight with Dau for any reason and did not want to see the Pandavas distressed. Before the war when Dau said he was going on pilgrimage, I was ready for it. Even though he knew why and he wanted to solve my dilemma. The love we brothers shared is very rare to find on this earth.

Pandavas were distressed because it was a difficult war. Kauravas strength was 11 Akshauhini armies (one Akshauhini had thousands of elephants, chariots ,horses and infantry) Bhishma, Drona, Duryodhana, Ashwathama and the great Karna, and other than these, their friends. And on this side 7 Akshauhini and a few friendly kings. Because of friendship, Shiva and Hanuman were on the Pandava side, but in a war, strength came before religion and mood. This is why the rules for a war had to be decided, this was not politics, it was a physical war.

"Dau, even my mind wants me to turn a blind eye, like you or Shiva, but sometime else. See you soon." I thought of this but couldn't say it. Dau hugged me and ran his hand on my head, and I remembered the day when to avoid the noise I would get lost in the jungle to meditate. Only one person used to know and Dau always used to hug me like this.

But now one day before the war strength couldn't be given, all friends had been contacted. All of them had arrived. Without telling anyone I had called Bhim's son

Ghatotkach and an elephant named Ashwathama.

This elephant was given birth a while back, by me in a forest. The elephant rider asked me to name him, I named him this. Now I remembered him. Strength could not have been increased, but the enemy's could have been lessened. And this was what I was doing, through tricks and wit, the rest I left on history.

When the messengers were being sent to friends asking for help, I remembered someone who the Pandavas had also forgotten. I had said anything can happen at any time, like me he had nothing to do with this war, but he would have come and would have supported the Kauravas because he had to take revenge from me. Even I didn't know why I was escaping him. It was time for Jarasandh and I wanted to send a message to the Kauravas, telling them of the strength of the Pandavas. If I would have killed him , nothing would have happened, because I was not fighting the war. So I disguised myself and took Bhim to Magadh where there was a fight competition happening. Jarasandh was a strong warrior and defeating him was impossible without strategy. Both me and Bhim could have been recognised that it is why I took Bhim as a participant and I hid in the crowd.

Jarasandh was defeating one warrior after the other, when on my signal Bhim challenged him. Jarasandh recognised Bhim but he knew nothing would happen to him. He could not have thought about me. When Bhim made eye contact with me I tore a straw from the middle and threw both the pieces in different directions. Bhim immediately tore Jarasandh from the middle and threw the two equal parts. Jara could not be joined now. While dying, his eyes were looking for me and we had eye contact for a few seconds. I gave the throne to his son and a rightful funeral to Jarasandh. One obstacle had been removed, but there were many more.

One day before the war, I went to the Kaurava camp to ask them about how they were, and I met almost everyone, with all my love, there was no evil motive behind it.According to the rules, the war had to happen between equal soldiers, from sunrise to sunset, after that they ask about each other and heal wounds. I had added this rule because I had to end hatred after the war. In the end I went to Karna's tent.

"Madhav, I was just thinking about you, look Bhishm Pithamah has kept me away from the war and has given me the task to give water to the soldiers." There was sadness in his voice. I knew about Bhishm's order, that till he was alive, Karna would not fight. And he was desperate to put down Arjuna. But Bhishma knew something else that only me and Kunti knew. This secret of the last generation was told to me by Durvasa. Karna was Kunti's eldest son.

This was all Durvasa's doing. He was impressed by a young woman and had given her a boon that she could have a child with any one she liked. A 16 year old girl and without understanding her mental condition, lit a fire. Later this story was tried to be explained as a hymn, Kunti tested the boon, called the Sun God and got pregnant. She left this baby to float on the river and then later a charioteer brought up this child. Kunti's son, the king of Aryavart, became a Charioteer's son but he was also the son of the Sun god, he could not have been hidden. I think till today, that day was it Kunti's youthful wish or Durvasa's desire, because getting pregnant is through one process only, a physical relation.

Arjuna didn't know and he used to taunt me by saying why I loved Karna so much.

Arjuna's hatred and jealousy for Karna used to come out as abuse-- charioteer's son etc. I had to scold Arjuna too. I did not tell them, otherwise the Pandavas would have given everything to Karna, and he would have given it to Duryodhana.

Karna on the other hand was living in a state where he wanted to prove he was a better warrior than Arjuna and the one day they were opposite each other, he was insulted due to his birth. Duryodhana saved his honour by making him Ang-raj which gave him respect. That is why he was the most important person for Karna, even if he was wrong.

If one recognises his power and does not get the respect he deserves then the anger, jealousy enter the mind which is dangerous. Karna had to deal with being a Charioteer's son all his life. Even I did not leave this, he was the ideal husband for Draupadi, Arjuna was after him, he would have shot the fish's eye, but I had signalled Drauapdi to say no. And Draupadi too, rejected to marry him in a full gathering, even before he shot an arrow. Parushuram had also cursed him, because of him being a charioteer's son without looking at his knowledge and skills. I knew Karna better than Arjuna. He turned this insult into the other direction, there was no one as charitable as him on this planet and never will be.

But that day I was trying to do an impossible task.

I brought Karna outside the camp where nobody could hear us. There I told him the history of his birth.I was expecting pain and grief on his face but he was the Charitable Karna , he just had a sarcastic smile on his face, the one that people never showed me. And for the first time I had no answer.

"Madhav, sometimes you fill me with surprise. Today an evening before the war why tell me this? Your Pandava love is unbreakable and you are respected. But however much I might love you, I don't have the courage or the mental state to give you anything."

I was shocked- "I am not asking for any charity, I am just telling you the truth."

"Madhav, do you know why you are called God ? It's not

that what you do anybody else cannot do, but you do it at the right time and place and we do it at the wrong time" said Karna, staring at me.

I said "So what is this time right for?"

Karna "Lord, it is the time of hope, maybe after listening to this I might leave Duryodhana's side and your beloved Arjuna would be safe. But I am outside the war, everything is fine."

"Karna, I was just…"

"Madhav, you know everything, would you want me to not repay Duryodhana, I deceive him and go down in history and get insulted ?The insults of this life were less ? or should I be called a traitor even after death ?... Now whatever you say."

He stopped for a second and it was the hardest time of my life.

"Madhav, I am also your brother, if you tell me I will remove myself from the war and become a charioteer in the Pandava army like you, but then tell me how I will face Duryodhana or take my eyes in charity."

After this I said nothing. I hugged him and was leaving, but turned and said - "Karna, you will remain great, whatever decision you take, just meet your mother once, meet Kunti."

Karna - "You are very stubborn Krishna, you will shoot your arrows through mother. Try.But Madhav, don't tell this to anyone." He looked at my face and said, "Otherwise the Kauravas will surrender, Yudhishthir will give the throne to me and I will become the king."

I said -"so?"

"Madhav, I don't want to be the king and once this comes out in the open, Kunti's motherhood will be disgraced?"

He said this and left. I stood there trying to understand the meaning of being a Suryaputra.

Later Kunti told me that Karna had promised her that Kunti's five sons would live, but between Arjuna and Karna, only one. He fulfilled the promise, after entering the war and after seven days having had the opportunity he didn't kill Yudhisthira, Bhim, Nakul or Sahadeva. The story of his and Arjuna's war later.

In my self created trapeze, I don't want to leave anything because that could tangle the ropes and there were quite a few of them. One day, in jest I asked all the soldiers how many days they would take to end the war alone. From Bhishma to Arjuna everybody answered according to their capabilities. I was also judging their egos and according to that I was creating their roles in my head. At that moment Bhima's grandson, Ghatotkcha's son, Barbirik arrived. He had no ego, but he asked for permission to fight. The Pandavas got excited to get another warrior but I stopped him. My spies had told

me about his skills. He had attained mastery through meditation. "One day" he said. He would end it in a day and people were shocked. He was right, he had 3 boons- First, with which he could target all his enemies. The second one to target all that he had to save and the third was destruction of the targeted enemies. In reality, Pandavas would have won but that would have happened without them fulfilling their duty and I didn't want that to happen. But he had made a promise to his mother that he would only fight from the weaker side and according to him the Pandavas were weak due to their army. He wasn't wrong, but he hadn't counted me. My problems increased. I agree that I was a little unfair to Bhim and Hidimba's family, but I had no other way.

I told him to demonstrate — I told him to tie all the leaves of the Peepal tree and destroy them.When he closed his eyes to meditate, I picked a leaf and hid it under my foot. He tied all the leaves together with an arrow and then the arrow came over my foot and stopped.He asked me to lift my foot, but before I could do that, the arrow had gone through my foot, targeted the leaf and the other arrow had saved it and the third destroyed it. I knew it. Pandavas' happiness was reflected in their excitement. I had to stop Barbarik.I reminded him of his promise that if he fought from the Pandavas side, the Kauravas would become weak and then he would have to switch sides. So this way he will have to switch sides, and thus he should stay away from the war for the Pandavas and sacrifice himself. I promised him immortality, at least he would be remembered. But he too gave me something, a wound in my foot, the same foot Durvasa had left from becoming a weapon. Jara's arrow had to hit right here.

After finishing this I reached the camp and got a message that someone was waiting for me near the lake.I reached there and was shocked, Dau was sitting under a tree drinking. When he was happy, Som Rasa was his companion. Seeing Dau like that made me a little jealous, I was busy with other people's problems and here he was. Looking at me he got up and hugged me and said - "Kanha, why do you torture yourself, you don't have to take all the problems, take some rest."

Dau used to say this quite often but today I got irritated, But before I could say something he said "Look who I got for your rest."

Suddenly from behind the tree 15-20 women came and I forgot everything. My Gopikas, my companions. All of them were old like me but the same shape, the same face. I hugged them and the tears washed away all the pain.

" All of you here, how." I asked.

" Kanha, you never came, when Dau told us that you were nearby we thought we should go and meet you before we die so that our souls find peace."

" When was I seperate from you."

One of them said— "You haven't stopped making stories, but now you are not Kanha, you are Dwarkadhish."

I understood Dau was taking his anger out on me through them.

But my eyes were searching for something, they understood it.

"She didn't come, you left her Kanha, Radha didn't leave you, you will have to go to meet her."

I was startled.

The other one said "He still feels shy after hearing her name, Dau, but Radha has sent a message."

My excitement was obvious- "What."

" Radha has said that you had left her hand and gone that day. And since then you have been lost, in the forest, in the city, you have left the flute and have taken the Chakra.When everything is over, come, you will find me under the same tree from where you had left. When you get tired don't hesitate, my touch will give you rest."

They said this, turned and went back. I held my hand out to stop them and tried to say something but Dau stopped me. I turned and fell in his arms and started crying.

Balram ran his hand on my head, like he used to do in our childhood. Without any anger he said- "This war is going to give you pain and when you will be in pain,I will be in pain too. Go and fulfill your duty, Make the worthy win and... Use your power and love for the worthy, wisely."

Dau left and I was absolutely alone, I was not this alone even under water with Kaalia. Till today I am trying to understand the "worthy." Since the beginning of the war Bhishma had adorned the angry form, like he wanted to end everything in 2-3 days, but his arrows stayed away from the Pandavas. Not only did I understand this but also Duryodhana. Spies told me that Duryodhana had openly wounded Bhishma and Dronacharya with his words and had doubted their mind, but what could he do, he couldn't fight without them. Bhishma's anger had landed the Pandavas in a frenzy.

This had its effects on the camp which I saw in the evening when Yudhisthira taunted Arjuna and said

"Parth, you are the world's best archer, what are you doing? What is the use of your Gandiva."

During the time of Gita I also wanted to say that Arjuna you practiced all your life to be the best archer and when it's time to use these skills you are running away. I had turned things around and said them because I did not want him to be discouraged.

Yudhisthir shot a direct arrow and said "When Pitamah finishes the entire army, will you then thread your bow ?" The king inside the brother was rising.

Arjuna had pledged that whoever insults his Gandiva, he

would kill that person. Till this time I was not there, spies told me and requested me to help.

When I reached Arjuna was aiming his Gandiva at Yudhistir. I was just about to laugh, I was trying to make them win and they were fighting like children, at the wrong time. People were calming Arjuna and Yudhisthira was sitting shocked like he used to get after his childish behaviour.

"Arjuna", he lowered the bow after listening to my voice. And guilt was clear on his face.

" I have sinned, I took arms against my elder brother, I was under oath, but even then, I have no path now, I will kill myself."

On the day of the Gita he was distracted, today he was foolish.

My voice had anger "Why do you brothers take oaths and pledges on everything? Have the power to fulfill them too. Go, Arjuna, Kill Yudhisthira and then kill yourself, I will declare the end of the war and Draupadi you live in your husband's love.I am going."

I had just turned to leave when Draupadi came in front of me and said "Tying my hair was your duty Keshav and I had asked for war on the basis of your powers not the unstable minds of the Pandavas. When you decided to not fight, I was upset, but you wanted to give these brothers some confidence. Otherwise my hair would have been bathed in the Kaurava blood by now."

" Krishnaa, Your pledge during your dishonour has led to the spilling of blood of so many people. This was not right but you still are not able to overcome revenge." As soon as I said this Draupadi looked me in the eye and said "Then take revenge for the insult of your love, Krishna."

And before leaving she looked at her husbands mockingly and said "If you want to win, fix your arms and weapons." She had never talked about her love openly. Pandavas like always were sitting lost.

I told Arjuna that if he had to fulfill his oath then he should do two things. Abuse your elder brother because abusing your elder brother is like killing him. Arjuna hesitated but then he did this and was ready to kill himself. To please his soul I said, self- praising is like suicide. When the conditions of his oath were over I told them to think of the problem named Bhishma.

The next day Arjuna was very excited but he was running away from Bhishma.As soon as Bhishma used to come in front of Arjuna, his arrows lost their target. I was continuously reminding Arjuna and on the other side Bhishma had finished half of the Pandava army.

My patience was about to break by afternoon and I broke my oath. Without asking Arjuna I had taken the chariot in front of Bhishma's chariot and was waiting for Arjuna to understand the signal but his arms had become jelly.

I experienced anger that day, which was going to happen multiple times.

In front of my eyes, because of Arjuna, I was seeing helpless soldiers being killed, but neither Arjuna or Bhishma were worried about that. In order to protect each other they were sacrificing others.

I jumped out of the chariot, I was without any arms but since childhood I had fought with bare hands. I picked up a wheel from a broken chariot nearby and ran towards Bhishma. Before I could reach there, I could feel a hand on my legs, Arjuna was pleading "You please don't break your promise, Madhav." Bhishma had also dropped his weapons, the war had come to a stand still.

Bhishma folded his hand and kneeled in front of me and Arjuna was holding my leg. One warrior wanted me to hit him and free him and the other was still in his emotions. If one army general did this to the other army general, it would have been a surrender, but I was just a charioteer. I did not want to defeat Bhishma this way and insult him and why would I do that ? Maybe Draupadi's love yesterday had shaken me up.

I threw the wheel, embraced Bhishma and sent him back. I did not say anything to Arjuna because after seeing Bhishma I knew why his arrows were not hitting him. Bhishma did not want to attack a chariot on which I was sitting. My heart was filled with respect for him and I knew Arjuna was only alive because of me.

But this way the war would never end, Pitamah had the boon of choosing his death. One had to ask him for his death.

In the night, I took the Pandavas and went to Bhishma's tent, hiding from Duryodhana. Bhishma knew why I had come, he had seen life more than all of us. The incident in the day had told him that it was time for him to leave. He said "Madhav, What can I do for you?"

"Father, Don't solve my problem, solve the Pandavas' problem."

"What is their problem?"

"They won't say it in front of you."

Bhishma smiled- "Madhav, Today in the day you had solved the problem, both theirs and mine."

"Pitamah, they will have to solve this problem on their own."

The five brothers were standing mute.

"Madhva, go, rest. Tomorrow's sun will bring something new. A woman is very eager to meet me from the last life." We turned and before I left the camp Bhishma said to me "Even if it is a half woman."

After reaching the camp I told Yudhistir to call Shikhandi. In the last birth Amba, with her three sisters, were abducted by Bhishma from the king of Kashi for the Kuru king Vichitraveerya. He himself had taken an oath to never marry or become the king, he had done this to make Satyavati and his father Shantanu's marriage happy so that their son becomes the king.

Two sisters stayed but Amba told about her wishes and said that she loved someone else. Bhishma sent her back but Shalya insulted her because Bhishma had kidnapped her. Amba asked Bhishma to marry her, which was not possible. Amba pledged to take revenge from Bhishma and welcomed death.

In this life she was born half woman in Drupad's house as Shikhandi.

To defeat the Kaurava all the weapons were with Drupad, you can call this the working of destiny that Shikhandi remembered her past life and even about her revenge from Bhishma and his death.

Bhishma was a warrior and never attacked women, and he knew Shikhandi. That day he had saved us and had fulfilled Shikhandi's life. It would not have happened without his own will.

Duryodhana was doubtful about our meeting, he tightened the circle around Bhishma. But my chariot by the end of the day reached him.

Before Bhishma's strike, Shikhandi stood in front of Arjuna, Bhishma looked at me and smiled, he signalled me with his eyes and kept his bow down. Shikahndi's arrow wounded him and Arjuna's arrow made Bhishma drop to the ground. That day it was seen that Bhishma was the true warrior and till date Arjuna's arrow, like toys, could not reach his bow. Today no arrow was cut, his eyes were stuck on me till he fell. The war stopped. Everyone reached near him. 105 brothers who had played in his lap, each of them was crying. All of them were united in sadness.

The arrows were through the body, removing them was impossible and because of this half his body was hanging. I made a bed of arrows for his body to lie on. Bhishma could speak and he told us his day to die was after a few days. After making a circle of security around him I told everyone to leave and I sat there holding his hand for a while. Why do I get all the painful moments ?

I was waiting for two people. Shikhandi came, folded his hands in front of Bhishma and cried, maybe because of guilt. Nobody won over Bhishma, he freed everyone from himself.

The second person came later and I hid myself but he knew I was somewhere nearby.Karna came, bowed before Bhishma and he gestured to him to come near his face.

Karna sat on his knees and Bhishma asked him "How are you, Karna ?"

Karna- "Alive in your shadow."

Bhishma- "Karna, I never gave you respect, you know why ?"

Karna kept listening.

Bhishma held his hand and said "After me there is no better warrior than you in the whole of Aryavart. But I wanted you to stay away from this war and Duryodhana, because…"

" because I am Kunti's son."

Bhishma was shocked- "So Krishna has told you. Forgive me if you can for all the words I spoke to you. So what is your decision?"

" Pitamah, I have promised mothcr Kunti that hcr fivc sons will live."

Bhishma looked at him lovingly "You are the son of the Sun god, you will spread light even after burning. Go fulfill your duty of being a friend, when everything will have ended, Charitable Karna will be remembered."

Karna bowed to him and got up. His eyes found me and he left towards the darkness.

The next day was heavy for the Pandavas. Karna landed as danger and Dronacharya's skills shocked the army. The next two days had coloured the soil of Kururkshetra, red. With Bhishma no plans had to be made, we just had to tell him the problem. But now the situation was different. On one side Duryodhana was taunting everyone and was blaming Dronacharya for sympathising with the Pandavas. Drona took a pledge that he would defeat any one Pandava.

Everyone was cautious and alert. And me and Arjuna, had gone far away from the war zone. That day Arjuna had to show all his archery skills. I had only one doubt in my head and it was proven truthful.

In the evening when we returned to the Pandava camp there was silence for the dead. As soon as we entered I understood everything because Draupadi and Subhadra were crying in one corner and the Pandavas were sitting with their heads bowed down. Seeing me, Subhadra held me,her cry filled the sky.

I ran my hand on my sister's head and said "He was born for this day."

Arjuna suddenly realised and asked "Where is Abhimanyu ?"

Then he was told that while he was stuck in the war Drona had made the Chakravyuh. Nobody had the knowledge to enter it, but Abhimanyu had learnt it from the conversation between me, Subhadra and Arjuna. My sister was also a warrior and was interested in warfare. When this challenge came, Arjuna wasn't there and Abhimanyu insisted on going.

He had said that he didn't know the art of coming out of the Chakravyuh. The other Pandavas said that they would follow him inside and get him out. And this is where they faultered.

Abhimanyu was Arjuna's son and my disciple, his speed and others' speed were different. He entered the Chakravyuh like an arrow and till the time the rest reached, Drona had closed all the entry points.

Then the maryada (dignity) was broken. Abhimanyu was killed ruthlessly by 6-7 warriors. He fought but not thinking about his age, the same warriors who had left the Pandava brothers alive, killed Abhimanyu.

It was truthful to say, that in wars things like these happen, but this wasn't war it was just ghastly murder. Somewhere in my deep subconscious mind Subhadra's tears had shaken me up. It had added fuel to Draupadi's fire and I took Draupadi and Subhadra out from the camp, for Abhimanyu's cremation, because I was worried that Uttara would insist on becoming a Sati.She could be stopped after a lot of persuasion. It was important because in her womb was the future of Bharat, Abhimanyu's son, who was later called Parikshit.

I should not have done it but now I had pledged to break all promises, without telling anyone, because after Bhishma, Kauravas had forgotten Dharma. Dronacharya was on the pay of the Kauravas and Karna was under the debts of Duryodhana. And rest every one's mind had the shadow of Shakuni. Their friends had their own stories of revenge from someone or the other. Arjuna had an old enmity with Jaydrath, and he had taken all revenge by killing Abhimnayu. But he made a mistake. Abhimanyu was dear to me.

Now deceit was going to take new forms. The great war was now going to be fought with brain and not with arms. I was not worried about what would happen in the future, and nor was I like the victors who wanted to write their praises in history. I had to establish Dharma and had to show people that in danger, wit can defeat deceit as well. After doing it there is no reason to protect it and no one tries to stop it before. Even today the human brain does this.

I was thinking of the war plans and on the other hand Arjuna was increasing my work. He pledged that before the sunset the next day he would kill Jaydrath or else he would kill himself. What could I have said, now I had to think how to get Jaydrath in front of Arjuna, in a war zone this huge, it was easy for him to hide, and we would spend the entire day looking for him.

But I knew what nobody else knew-- the nature of ego. False Ego resides in the world's most scared human,he trembles from within during danger while creating false bravado, and after the danger is over, his ego comes back.

The next day the exact thing happened, it was afternoon, wherever Arjuna asked me I took the chariot in chase. Jaydrath was not found. Even I wanted to teach Arjuna a lesson, that do not take oaths in anger, take oaths with a calm mind, or else you will always require Krishna to help you. One day when there will be no Krishna, you will only get defeat. When there were two hours left for the sun to set I could see tiredness and hopelessness on the faces of the Pandavas.

I stopped the chariot and gave the nearest horseback soldier some orders. Satyaki had disguised these soldiers and had kept them with me. He ran from one to the other and then to the third and within an hour the people standing in the desert had heard my orders.

Here the search was on and the Pandavas because of their ego were not asking for my help. I let it happen. All of them were the same, after all the Pandavas were also the Kauravas.

Suddenly, the sun began to set in the west, nobody noticed that today it was happening a little earlier. As soon as the darkness spread a voice echoed "Arjuna you lost, you could not kill me, now give me your life and save your insult." Jayadrath brought his chariot right in front of Arjuna and behind him were the Kauravas, ready to witness Arjuna's death.

Arjuna was about to keep his bow down when I said "String the bow, Parth."

Arjuna, like always, was caught in a bind "But now, I can't shoot, it's after sunset."

"Don't be stupid, war is won not by dying but by killing." They made me say the Gita during the war "Look there."

The sun was visible again in the west. Everyone was shell shocked, Arjuna's arrows killed Jaydrath. People took this to be my miracle and started chanting my name, adding another layer of Godliness on me.

People are either too innocent or too scared, I could never decide, maybe when wit cannot understand then God is needed, to take the responsibility on his shoulder. But this was not that huge a miracle.

On the West of Kurukshetra there were desert peaks, one set of army on camels and horses was ready there, the last group of army of Dwarka, which was the first step to go to Dwarka. The chain of horseback soldiers I had prepared yesterday were instructed today, one hour before sunset to release all camels and horses in the desert. There was a huge gush of sand that rose from behind the peaks, it hid the sun and the rest was hidden by the dust of ego, creating darkness. Till the time Jaydrath showed himself, the sand had settled and the sun had risen again.

This was a balance between Math and nature, hearing the language of time as a childhood skill. Arjuna's mind was not calm. Loss had drawn a curtain on his brain. After the revenge was taken his doubts came forward "Madhav, you can do anything, let me meet Abhimanyu once."

I was shocked. "Impossible, win over your grief, the war is not over." Arjuna cried for a long time and I needed him for the war.

How can I make him meet the dead ? Something had to be done. I told him to close his eyes and to meditate and I kept my finger at the same spot as Shiva's third eye. After a while Arjuna's body was listless and he was sweating. When he regained consciousness he was sad, but quiet. I did not ask him but he was eager to tell me.

He told me he had reached the war with me, and there he saw Abhimanyu. With 15 soldiers, he came to me fighting and said "King, Stay away from here, this is a war, you will get wounded. I tried to tell him I was his father but he didn't recognise me."

"Arjuna, relations on this earth are limited and are born in our life. Abhimanyu is free from all of this now. We will have to wait for our freedom."

Arjuna had remembered Shiva, but had not thought of Indra that is why he was always in trouble. I had only sent him to sleep in meditation.Everything else was in his unconscious mind: My existence, Abhimanyu in his war form which he could not see in Kurukshetra and had imagined it in his mind, death had separated him so the pain of that, in the form of Abhimanyu's form.

These games are played within every mind and we call them dreams. I had shown Arjuna a divine dream. But one question had arisen in my mind, would Subhadra have done the same ? A long war takes pain till far and the mental state gets worse. Now I wanted to finish this fast and bring balance and equality in life.

Defeating Dronacharya was difficult, but I had a hack.

Struggle was with one Pandava, and his own vision about himself. Yudhistira could lose his kingdom and wife at a game of dice, but his ego for his truthfulness was high,even if his truth was of no use.

But I scared all the Pandavas by saying that till Drona was alive, forget about winning the war. I had made it personal. Drupad's son Drishtadyumna ,wanted to kill Drona in order to avenge his father and Arjuna was waiting for Karna. Both of them got ready but making Dharamraj Yudhisthir lie was an arduous task. So I decided to tell him the truth. I brought Ashwathama the elephant to the war zone the next day and put him in a place where his death was inevitable. I told the soldiers that after his death there should be noise and the noise should be "Ashwathama is dead."

Guru Drona was busy in war with Arjuna. He heard it but did not stop. I stopped Arjuna and shouted "Guru, let us stop the war, your son is no more."

Drona said in a loud voice "Till I don't hear it from Yudhistir, I will not believe it. Don't distract me, Krishna." I had shot an arrow in the darkness, it would have worked but Drona had taught these 105 brothers, he was aware about everything and he obviously knew me. The wounds of Bhishma's defeat were fresh.

Making Yudhishtir say it, meant having a whole discussion, which we didn't have time for. 7Because then Drona would have realised the lie. I called Yudhisthira's chariot near me. The War stopped for sometime. The Pandavas and I surrounded him and requested that he tell Drona this. Like I feared he wanted to know the truth and said "Take him to Gurudev, he will see it and believe it."

There was no time for all this. Drona would have suspected something. I ordered- "Yudhishtira, not every moment is for your lazy behaviour, it is a war, do as I say."

He was a little scared and hearing me shout he said "What do I have to say ?"

"The truth, and that too loudly so that your voice can be heard by Guruvar, and the truth is that Ashwathama the elephant is dead."

I could not have given Yudhistira more time than this. I dragged him and got him to my chariot from where Drona was visible.

I shouted "Gurudev, you are not understanding

Ashwathama is dead, listen to him."

Yudhishtira was shivering but he said it because I was standing behind him - "Ashwathama hato hata:"

He said the second sentence as well, "Naro va Kunjro va", but it got suppressed by the sound of my conch and the other conches blowing.

Drona dropped his weapons. I walked to him. He said "It is the truth, Krishna?"

"Gurudev, if I say that he was not your son but an animal will you fight again? So much attachment to life and offspring, it doesn't suit learned men like you and it corrupts them from both the path and the power. You think for yourself."

I turned and Drona bowed his head and sat. Drishtduymna cut his head and his head fell near me, and it felt like his eyes were saying "I am free from all attachments."

Pandavas were happy, Yudhisthira was a little angry, I sent Draupadi, if the mother's warmth could not then a wife could give him some consolation. Either way I did not want to waste my mental power on such useless things because tomorrow was going to bring a new storm — Karna.

The anger which had accumulated for ages in Karna burst like a volcano, over the Pandava army. Karna defeated all the brothers and let them live, because of his promise to Kunti. I was protecting Arjuna from facing him, because I had seen the reality the first day itself.

Arjuna's arrows had pushed Karna's chariot behind and when Karna shot his arrows, Arjuna's chariot just moved a little. The words "Great" left my mouth.

Arjuna's jealousy woke him up and he said "I don't understand Madhav. Why do you love the charioteer's son so much? I pushed his chariot so far and you said nothing, he just moved my chariot a little, and you are praising him so much."

My voice turned stern "Arjuna, why do you keep calling him a charioteer's son and what do you wish to prove by that? You don't have to defeat his caste, you have to defeat him. Abuses will not reach him like arrows and that has already happened. Every insult has filled his arrows with anger and revenge, just for you."

Arjuna still did not get it. His jealousy was decreasing his strength and wit.

"Arjuna, don't be blind, he is alone, and here on your chariot, you have me,and carrying the weights of the three worlds is Hanuman. Even after all this weight he moved your chariot, think."

Arjuna did not think that Karna could be the reason for his death. To lessen his strength and to make Arjuna win a lot of people were trying and working.

The king of Madra, Shalya, was the maternal uncle of the Pandavas, when he left for the war, the Kauravas made camps for his safety on the way and taking them to be the Pandavas blessed them with the victory in the war.Shalya wanted to change sides but I stopped him and told him to be Karna's charioteer but I gave him one task.

"Uncle, Me and you both are doing the same work, protecting the warrior and the horses, but there will be a difference, both the warriors are great. You have to bring his moral down and I have to increase the moral of mine."

A charioteer does not only drive the chariot, he is also the guide for directions, sometimes even shows the path, boosts the warrior, along with the language of the horses, he understands the mental state of the warrior as well. The war between Karna and Arjuna was actually changed by the two charioteers and their different behaviours.

Shalya for the entire duration was discouraging Karna but he was silent. He knew this was all my doing, he just wanted an equal war with Arjuna, but I knew in an equal fight, Arjuna would be finished. Arjuna didn't know Karna was fighting all alone on his strengths, Arjuna was fighting along with me, by becoming Narayana's weapon. He and I did not only have a relationship with feelings but also we were joined by the blessings of Shiva and the third thread tying us together was the chariot itself.

At the time of Khandavaprastha, after a lot of practice he had gotten the Gandiva and the chariot Kapidhwaj from Nagraj Takshak. The fire wanted freedom from snakes, the terror of fire was finished by rain because Indra was Takshak's friend. I was with the Pandavas when they reached Khandavaprastha to make Indraprastha. My relation with the snakes and Indra was from Vrindavan. But this time I did not give it a chance. It was shocking, For Indra's son I was rendering Indra unsuccessful. The flag of the chariot had Hanuman's blessings.

Arjuna did not understand this till the end of the war. On the eighteenth day after the sunset, I told Arjuna to get down from the chariot. As soon as he stepped down I let loose the four horses. When I jumped out of the chariot, the chariot began to burn. Arjuna was shocked.

"What just happened, Madhav."

"Parth, where was the chariot. Karna had already destroyed it. Shiva and Hanuman were balancing it." I deliberately did not take the credit myself.

That day Arjuna realised that Karna was no ordinary warrior and Arjuna was in a privileged position in front of him. Karna was not only alone but also cursed.

He had Parushuram's curse on him and before the war, Arjuna's father Indra had disguised himself and had taken Karna's shield and earrings as alms. These were the powers of Karna. And right before the war, they were snatched from him.

I had made him waste his strongest weapon on Ghatotkach.

If he would have defeated Arjuna even after all this, he would have become the Dharma. My fears were coming true, Arjuna was not able to face him any longer. I had to use a trick again. I told Arjuna to break the wheels of his chariot. When he fell and asked Shalya for help, Shalya did not help.

At the same time I told Arjuna to attack, Karna tried really hard, to remember the chant for the weapon that he had saved for Arjuna. But Parushuram's curse did not let that happen. Karna lost.

Arjuna thought that he defeated him, maybe he was caught with guilt, attacking a weapon -less Karna, but I knew who had actually won.

In the night I conducted his funeral myself. Without the Pandavas and without Kunti.

In the middle of this people were fulfilling their oaths. The Kaurava army was on the verge of defeat. All the brothers were dead. Dushasan's body had been torn by Bhim and his blood had been sent to Draupadi and she had tied her hair. Shakuni and his sons were killed. Now it was just Duryodhana and Ashwathama, Kritvarma, Kripacharya and their soldiers. My interest in this bloodshed was now over but some work was still unfinished.

Gandhari called Duryodhana and she told him to visit her naked so she could by opening her eyes and with her power could make his body a shield. I met him on the way and I told him that he could not go to his mother naked. He covered himself from the waist to the thighs with a leaf.

When Gandhari opened her eyes she was shocked. She understood that it was my trick.

Duryodhana hid in the lake and when he was found then Yudhisthira asked him to choose a warrior for the war. Ego led to defeat but now Duryodhana did not want to live.

He fought with Bhim. If it had not been the question of life and death then the sheer beauty of the duel was worth watching. I indicated to Bhim and hit my thigh with my hand. Bhim in the next moment hit Duryodhana's thigh ,the same weak spot that I had made him cover. Duryodhana was dead.

But a new trouble came on my head. At that same time Dau appeared. He was watching from afar and when Bhim broke Duryodhana's thigh, Dau got angry and took out his mace. (Gada)

" I will kill Bhim, he has broken the rules."

Dau and his mace, who could have stopped them. I had to use my entire strength to stop him "Dau, it is not our fight. All rules have been broken. There is nothing left to save, you leave it."

One after the other, the end to this story was nowhere

to be seen. We had absolutely forgotten one person, Aswathama. The last night of war when the Pandavas and I went towards the battle ground, Ashwathama created havoc in the Pandava camp. Drishtdyumna, Draupadi's sons and who knows how many soldiers were killed. He fell like the God of death himself and there was revenge in his heart. And in his anger he shot the Bhramastra, but I stopped him.

This weapon would have killed the next few coming generations. Ashwathama didn't know how to stop the weapon, so he turned the arrow towards the fetus in Uttara's womb. The fetus dies. I immediately got it delivered and resuscitated it. While roaming in the jungle along with learning other skills I had also learnt how to assist in labour.

This fetus was the future of Bharat - Parikshit

After securing the future of Bharat I turned towards Ashwathama. You call it a curse or a punishment, but he had lost his mental calm and this was his future.

The future has more, it is always there. Why be sad about what has happened and why fear about what hasn't happened, but my words did not lessen the guilt of the Pandavas specially Yudhistira's. The victory was feeling like a burden for them. Draupadi's hair had been tied but the colour from her face had drained, the loss of her sons had made her think about all the deaths.

"Sakha, what did I do ?"

I did not want to give her more pain at that time. I kept my hand on her face and said "You did not do it ,the wheels of time did."

The war had ended and the people were bearing the brunt of the royal desires.The Pandavas return was to a Hastinapur that was looming with death.

This was the result of a blind king's greed and desires. The hidden jealousy in his subconscious had birthed Duryodhana. But Dhitrashtra did not learn. While meeting the Pandavas he wanted to hug Bhim, I was shocked by his choice and I put an iron statue in front of him. The king's strength crushed the statue. That was for Bhim. I saved Bhim but I could not save myself.

Gandhari cursed me because of the death of her sons "Krishna, my brother was taking revenge from this world, I tried explaining both the father and the son. But you used to talk about love, look at these widows."

Gandhari's words were like poison "You tied one Sakhi's hair and opened the hair of so many others. Even you became a victim of desire. Now you will experience the same.

I am cursing you, your lineage will also kill each other and you will get a death like this, unknown."

I could have answered but I kept quiet. Gandhari said this and fell into a pool of guilt. She held my hand and cried- "Krishna, don't accept the curse, I was angry."

"No, mother, all of this is necessary."

I would be in need of this curse a few years later.

Before saying farewell I had to meet two people-- Vyas and Sanjay, whose vision had seen everything and who would narrate this story to the coming generations. What I had said to Arjuna, Sanjay knew that, the story Vyas was about to write, Sanjay knew that. He was telling what he saw but Dhitrashtra was not listening.

He was blind as was the whole Aryavrat had become the story of the blind and me Krishna, who was about to become God, was looking at time, helplessly.

Do Gods always stand on the pile of dead bodies ?

Maybe wars never end, if they are not fought with body and not enemies, then they would keep happening in our mind and brain. This was in Arjuna's mind before the war and now in Yudhistira's mind. His heart was soft, he was always caught in some tension, guilt was obvious after seeing such massive bloodshed. So many deaths because of a kingdom, his Dharma was not ready to accept it. But I was in no mood for a lecture. I took him to Bhishma.

He was learned, even if he could not follow it. Bhishma was hesitating in speaking in front of me.

"Pitamah, you have ruled a kingdom, I haven't. Now Yudhistira will require that knowledge." I pushed him forward and stood near Bhishma's head, keeping my hand on his forehead.

After Yudhisthira's troubles lessened, Bhishma told him everything from the religion of governance to the path of peace, politics, work, caste difference, etc. This exercise had opened multiple ways, if this conversation would have reached the people, they would have created their own stories, and this is exactly what happened. They just did not imagine, they added their stories like they did with me.

But Yudhistira was as lost as Arjuna had been. It was not his mistake. Both me and Bhishma said "Work in accordance with time,time is in hands of death, the importance of elements, Yoga, detachment and man is not the doer he is the nimitta, the medium. This was enough but then the question "Then who am I ?"

And mankind had to be taught, work and Dharma.

I said "कर्मण्येवाधिकारस्ते मा फलेषु कदाचन" and freed myself.

But normal people are way more lost than Yudhisthira, they can't see any unity between these arguments. Whether karma is time based or will based and who holds the responsibility for its results?If there is time and destiny that rules then why is there a feeling of sin and virtues in man and if action is man's decision then sin and virtue is a yoke to keep humans in control. These contradictions raise anxiety in a lot of minds and not everyone is capable of maintaining a balance. Most of the people find a way and they spend their lives in one dimension without questioning the contradiction. Sometimes people come across something that is opposite to their path and a disbalance happens.Keeping the mind calm and eyeing the dispute with equanimity makes a human a yogi, everyone otherwise is deranged.

When Yudhishthira seemed to be more lost and less like a yogi, I had to repeat what I did with Arjuna. But this time I didn't want to narrate the Bhagwat, I pressed Bhishma's hand softly and he said "Yudhisthira, All these lessons end where even Madhav's penance ends. I am tired. Krishna, you can tell him the rest."

Bhishma very easily put it on me, and now I had to become God on my own. I decided to put this on someone who is ahead of me- Shiva.

Everyone remembers him, fears him but nobody knows him, not as much as I do because the love we share is different from this world. I told Yudhisthira about the miracles of Mahadev and told him to surrender completely to him so that my tensions could end.

Bhishma's departure's time had arrived. He bowed in front of me and stopped his breath. As soon as he died Yudhisthira fainted. Later Vyas explained to him and asked him to prepare for the Ashwamedh yag. The next few days Yudhisthira looked less like a king and more like a student, constantly asking questions from whoever he met.

He tangled me in a new strand of Vaishnav Dharm and taking the chance I declared all the work and caste division wrong. In order to get the Shudras respect I had to tell Yudhisthira that qualities are not made by birth, the caste difference divides work and in this no one is the best. If a Shudra is my devotee, anyone insulting him is poor.

I had to say this because in the future weak humans would use my words to declare their superiority, and this was an antidote to the problem.

Before they could turn me into a Dharm Guru, I decided to leave. Not everything was great but I didn't want to intrude in their new kingdom. Although the Pandavas were a little lost. Dhritarashtra, Kunti, Vidur, Gandhari … all of them were ready to depart for the forest and Arjuna, being tired, was resting. Bhim was busy with his own exercise. Nakul and Sahdev were the remaining ones, but they had their own limits. But because of the Ashwamedha everyone had to get involved. I wanted them to do this on their own strength.

And I wasn't receiving any good news from Dwarka, either.

When I reached Dwaraka ,I saw that the usually calm and happy city was distressed. Even Daruk and Satyaki felt this. In some time I realised the problem. I told Daruk to take the chariot from within the town. Seeing me people welcomed me, but every house had a sense of gloom. There was one or the other member in the family who was part of the Narayani army. Either they died or returned wounded, and the entire army hadn't even returned. Every person had the same question reflecting in their eyes. I realised that I will have to answer this question or will have to try and make everyone forget the question and there was only one solution— love.

Even love can't happen with questions !

I saw someone standing on the entrance, hidden under a cloth. I remembered Kubja. She gestured to me to come. I told Daruk to go and walked towards her. She removed the cloth, and I was shocked. She was Kubja. Old but just as beautiful.

She stared at me and said "Will you keep turning everyone pretty or will you take care of yourself as well ?"

"What happened to me"

She said "Look at your face in the mirror. Whose war were you fighting, Kanha ? And now you will have to spread love, to wipe everyone's tears."

As soon as she said this, she turned and said "If need be, I am here."

For a second I thought of hugging her, but I stopped. Where did I get lost ,from playing the flute to spinning the chakra, leaving the raag behind to letting the blood flow, from establishing love in the world to ending hatred, where I was stuck. Suddenly, I remembered Radha and I slapped my forehead. After the war I could have gone to Vrindavan to meet Radha, but the political Krishna overpowered the loving Krishna and there was a wish to change the world even after witnessing that everyone was the same. In the human form even the divine gets lost.

While accepting Gandhari's curse I had said, I am god or human, but I am tied to everyone through an invisible thread. I am the one dead and I am the reason for hatred, I am love and the happiness to live, I am the one who has to endure all this.

Today in Dwaraka, I was the one who had to do everything — love, anger, depression, everything. Because I was the one who was in everyone. To do this nobody has to become god. One only has to extend the horizons of their mind and join every living animal and human, and then you can understand their language.

It took twenty years to normalise life in Dwarka. In the process all of us grew old. It had been a long time since I met Draupadi and Arjuna. The last time they came my mind was distracted from the troubles and for some days we just enjoyed it, without any tensions. Now

Draupadi doesn't hide her love for me and Arjuna was a part of me. Rukmini or some other queen used to join us sometimes. Raas was still hidden in me somewhere. Either way, the Yadav clan had me involved and busy in business and fights. They were prosperous. But I had forgotten a rule. People who work continuously are the people who stay healthy and I was the one who taught them about KarmaYog. But I didn't apply this to my own family. Maybe the web of time in order to fulfill the curse brought this on me.

The Yadav warriors couldn't farm, labour wasn't in their blood and there were no wars happening. Desire, Alcohol and ego led to internal quarrels and this was their daily routine. I tried really hard to stop them, banned alcohol and even gave them responsibilities but nothing much happened. Dau himself was a lover of alcohol and the new young warriors had started to think I was old.

Some of them had crossed the line, they tried to fulfill their bodily hunger by trying to enter the house of the 16,000 women.In retort they replied that Krishna had just tied the sacred thread but had not satisfied them.

I tried to punish them but some family members came in between. Even I was listening to the footsteps of time through my senses and I had no excitement to save anything. The times were about to change, for good or for the bad, change was inevitable, and I could hear it. I was the hurdle in the flow of time but it had to do its job.And because of this he left my existence for the end and tried searching for it's medium. For destiny finding a medium or for time to prove its existence is no big miracle. A small change in the human mind starts a chain which turns into a farsighted result.

She stared at me and said "Will you keep turning everyone pretty or will you take care of yourself as well ?"

"What happened to me"

She said "Look at your face in the mirror. Whose war were you fighting, Kanha ? And now you will have to spread love, to wipe everyone's tears."

As soon as she said this, she turned and said "If need be, I am here."

For a second I thought of hugging her, but I stopped. Where did I get lost ,from playing the flute to spinning the chakra, leaving the raag behind to letting the blood flow, from establishing love in the world to ending hatred, where I was stuck. Suddenly, I remembered Radha and I slapped my forehead. After the war I could have gone to Vrindavan to meet Radha, but the political Krishna overpowered the loving Krishna and there was a wish to change the world even after witnessing that everyone was the same. In the human form even the divine gets lost.

While accepting Gandhari's curse I had said, I am god or human, but I am tied to everyone through an invisible thread. I am the one dead and I am the reason for hatred, I am love and the happiness to live, I am the one who has to endure all this.

Today in Dwaraka, I was the one who had to do everything — love, anger, depression, everything. Because I was the one who was in everyone. To do this nobody has to become god. One only has to extend the horizons of their mind and join every living animal and human, and then you can understand their language.

It took twenty years to normalise life in Dwarka. In the process all of us grew old. It had been a long time since I met Draupadi and Arjuna. The last time they came my mind was distracted from the troubles and for some days we just enjoyed it, without any tensions. Now Draupadi doesn't hide her love for me and Arjuna was a part of me. Rukmini or some other queen used to join us sometimes. Raas was still hidden in me somewhere. Either way, the Yadav clan had me involved and busy in business and fights. They were prosperous. But I had forgotten a rule. People who work continuously are the people who stay healthy and I was the one who taught them about KarmaYog. But I didn't apply this to my own family. Maybe the web of time in order to fulfill the curse brought this on me.

The Yadav warriors couldn't farm, labour wasn't in their blood and there were no wars happening. Desire, Alcohol and ego led to internal quarrels and this was their daily routine. I tried really hard to stop them, banned alcohol and even gave them responsibilities but nothing much happened. Dau himself was a lover of alcohol and the new young warriors had started to think I was old.

Some of them had crossed the line, they tried to fulfill their bodily hunger by trying to enter the house of the 16,000 women.In retort they replied that Krishna had just tied the sacred thread but had not satisfied them.

I tried to punish them but some family members came in between. Even I was listening to the footsteps of time through my senses and I had no excitement to save anything. The times were about to change, for good or for the bad, change was inevitable, and I could hear it. I was the hurdle in the flow of time but it had to do its job.And because of this he left my existence for the end and tried searching for it's medium. For destiny finding a medium or for time to prove its existence is no big miracle. A small change in the human mind starts a chain which turns into a farsighted result.

At the time of birth, if someone says it in the new born's ear that there is no one better than him and if someone puts fuel in the fire then the attitude and ego turns into a mountain. And mountains don't listen to anyone. Every human does this on some or the other level, and mostly the conversation is one sided. One speaks, the other one doesn't listen and is lost in his own thoughts and is waiting for his turn. The mind hears only the decision that has been made. People like me get stuck in this but my job was to tell whoever uses it. Those who will melt the self and expand the consciousness will become Krishna.

And Dwarka's air had ego. Old warriors in the glory of the past, and the new ones in the greed of their wishes. One whole generation thought that I was stopping them from being kings. They wouldn't be able to become kings in Dwarka and I wasn't letting them expand outside Dwarka. I was against imperialism or else by performing the Ashwamedh yagya we would have become the rulers of the world and each of them a king.But the only end would have been unpleasantness.I had protected the new generation from the goriness of the Mahabharata war. But the seeds of dispute were long sown...

One day, long back, there was noise outside my father Vasudev's house. By the time I could reach there, Dau had already reached. When I entered the room I was shell shocked, Dau was holding Satraajit's throat. Satraajit was a Yadav king and was a few years older to Dau. The others were trying to meddle to save. I went near Dau and tried to stop him—

"What happened, Dau ?"

" Satraajit has gone beyond his limits."

"What has he done?"

"He is blaming you for the theft."

I understood it and pleaded with Dau to leave him. I quickly called for a meeting because I didn't want to talk alone and give way to rumours. In the gathering Satrjit blamed me for stealing. A few years back I had asked him to give the Syamantaka Gem to me. There was a belief that this gem brought prosperity to the Yadavs. Who would tell them that prosperity came through hard work. I had asked for the gem only to keep it safely but Satrajit thought I was displaying my powers. Dau and I left the topic.

And now after all these years, a new story. I tried to have ignorance towards the entire matter but I was looking at the Yadav clan, dividing. My stopping them wouldn't help. The more serious blame other than stealing the gem was way more serious. Satrajit said that I had killed his brother Prasanjit because I didn't get the gem. Calming down an angry Dau became a problem but I didn't want a family feud that day (I hadn't gotten the curse till then)

I promised everyone that I would find the gem and Prasen. But before that I had to understand the relation between the two. My spies told me every secret about Satrajit. Prasenjit was fond of hunting and very greedy about the gem. He very often used to wear the gem in his neck and showed it off. One day he went hunting and didn't return. But Satrajit wasn't ready to agree that he had taken the gem. Meanwhile, I became friends with Satyabhama. She knew about her father's stubbornness and his lies. Love was blossoming in the shadows of enmity!

There was no other way than to look for Prasen. Along with some friends I started searching the forest. After a few days, we found a human skeleton and my friends instantly recognised him as Prasen. We realised that maybe he became prey to the lion but what would a lion do with the gem, so who else was there. We didn't have to wait long. Reechraj (the head of the bear tribe) Jambawant's soldiers took us with them. Entry of humans in that area was prohibited and we were to be punished. At that moment a girl came up to him, and even in the shadows of danger I felt desire for her. Her beauty had evolved because between her hair the gem was glistening. Jambwanti ,was looking like the queen of gems. Satyaki understood everything and even though he was tied up he told me "Vasudev, their weapons are on our throats, don't focus on the daughter, take the gem, apologise and leave."

"Yes, Satyaki."

I requested the king and asked for the gem, and as expected he talked about the rituals and challenged us for a fight. I asked him to spare my friends and hospitality for them during the war. These were the same Reechs who had helped Ram fight against Ravana and had settled here, on the West coast. Every ruler of theirs was called Jambawant and all of them were devotees of Rama. The fight went on for 28 days and nobody won. During the night we rested and fought in the day. Slowly and gradually we became Jambawant's guest and there was an unsaid bud of love. I find myself in this situation quite sometimes, on the side of war, Dwaraka's reputation at stake, Satyabhama in anticipation and here a new love story is brewing. When Satyaki used to get tired of all these things he used to fold his hands and called me Natwar Maharaj. Now, when he said it to me I decided to end the war the next day. It was easy, I just had to tell Jambwant, I was Rama's avatar and I was pleased by his devotion to his duty. I had asked for forgiveness from Rama for this crime. But the promise that Jambawant had made was that I could not separate the gem from his daughter but I could take his daughter with me as my wife. I readily accepted it. Managing another wife was easier than managing the Yadavas. As soon as I reached Dwarka, I returned the gem to Satraajit and he guiltily gave me Satyabhama's hand in marriage. Satyabhama was the figure of fire, saying no to her was out of the question and she was going to be my co-warrior in the future. The story of the gem was over but it left the seeds of doubt behind. It just needed a spark in the future. This poison had entered the air in Dwarka. Time found one incident and he played his dice.

One sage had settled in a nearby jungle to meditate. Sambh and his friends tried to cross the line and tried to test him. They took Sambh dressed like a woman and tied an iron utensil to his belly and asked him whether it would be a girl or a boy. The question in itself was ugly and asking the sage this question was pure disgrace. The sage opened his eyes and cursed "This womb will give birth to iron and all of you will die because of it."

They got scared and destroyed the iron and spread it in the ground. They powdered it and there was one piece that was left that went to the sea. Neither Dau nor I knew about this. And when we did get to know, 36 years had passed since the Mahabharata. And that too nobody told me. Dau and I were used to going near nature and listening to the animals, farms, flowers.We had gone to Somnath Temple to meet Shiva. From there walking on the water bank we crossed Prabhas and there my hand touched the high growing grass. I had done this earlier as well but for the first time I felt a sense of pain. I saw my fingers were bleeding. I called Dau and he cleaned my wounds. Every blade of grass was equal to a spear. The iron quantity of this grass was more than usual.

When we saw the soil, it was rich with iron. It takes at least 3-4 monsoons for the iron in the soil to go into the grass.

Dau and I didn't tell anyone about this but our spies told us that the farmers said that nothing had grown on that land for the past 2 years. They told us about the sage and Dau and I went to meet him. The sage told us about the curse and said that if I wanted he could lessen the power of his curse. I looked at Dau and he nodded in the negative. Dau folded his hand and while getting up he said "Sage, now tell me the day as well ?"

He wrote something with his finger on the ground.

From that day onward Dau lost all interest in life. Revati Bhabhi complained about this but I knew the reason. I told Dau and got alcohol banned and called for a meeting in Prabhas. Due to addiction everyone came, some unwillingly, some didn't want to go too far and they stopped where the Aerak grass was growing. The ocean was not too far and there was a hill nearby where I took my horses and Balram got involved in drinking with the Yadava clan.

I was standing there and watching the extremes of the ocean and the commotion of alcohol and ego. I could see Balram's blue clothes, he was sitting far away near the ocean. After a while I saw some bodies getting tangled together. And suddenly among the brown and the blue clothed, a red volcano erupted. The only word that echoed in my brain was - 'Beginning of the end.'

I sat on my horse and ran down the hill. As soon as I reached there I saw the body of Kritverma and people had surrounded Satyaki. Satyaki was holding a blood smeared sword and before I could reach there the people attacked Satyaki and a fight started. Everyone was intoxicated and no one knew who they were killing. There was blood everywhere. Some people ran towards me but Pradyuman jumped in the middle. Someone attacked him on the head with a mace and he fell in front of me, dead.

Satyaki and then this, I didn't want to stop this game of death but I didn't want to end my clan with my own hands. But now ……

My finger started moving in a circle and soon the Chakra started to spin on my finger. There was a time when people stopped when they heard the chakra but today nobody stopped. Who was fighting with whom, nobody knew. The hatred had erupted. Those who didn't have weapons picked up pieces of Aerak Grass and turned them into spears.

I killed violently after that. I left the Chakra and took a fist ful of grass and threw them as spears. After a few hours where silence spread I found myself standing in between bodies. Daruk, crying himself, found me.

" What happened, Madhav?"

"This was supposed to happen, but where is Dau?"

Both of us started shouting 'Dau' and kept searching for him but in between the bodies he couldn't hear us. Suddenly I remembered Dwarka. I exchanged horses with Daruk and sent him to Hastinapur to give the message to Arjuna to take everyone from here. I had told everything about everyone to Daruk.

I was worried about the safety of Dwarka. I reached there and consoled my parents, told the remaining soldiers about their duty and told them to wait for Arjuna. I had told everyone to vacate Dwarka because a warriors-less Dwarka would have been an invitation for greed. I met Satyabhama and Rukmini and then left to look for Dau.

One and a half day had passed. After I returned, I went towards the sea and suddenly saw Dau sitting amidst the waves, inside the sea. Tides were swallowing him like a snake.

There was one wave, I thought it was Sheshnag but I don't know what it was but I didn't see Dau. I fell on my knees there and kept crying, alone and supportless. The water was coming nearer to land. I slowly got up and started to walk back. The sea bank ended, the path ended as well and I went and sat in the jungle. I sat with my back resting on a tree trunk, my feet one on the other, just like I used to in Vrindavan. I didn't want to live without Dau.

When we were looking for a secure place for the residents of Mathura, I liked this place and Dau performed a yagya for me on the banks. In the end he prayed to the water to move backwards so that we could establish a city there.I don't know if it was Dau's strength or his friendship, but the sea left enough space to build Dwarka. We started living there and whenever we used to go near the bank, specially on the way to Somnath he used to say-

"Krishna, never take living on land as fixed." "I understand, Dau, but right now everything is fixed. Do you see any danger?"

He kept his hand on my shoulder and said—

" No, not from outsiders but from our own and on the land we are living."

"Who, Dau ?"

"This sea, the amount of help he has given, he will return to take it back."

I was thinking today was the day, I was crying for my brother and was praying to some unknown God to stop the waters till Arjuna arrives. Forgive me for anything I might have done wrong. A hopeless man can only pray.

I slept and I kept sitting like that. Suddenly my eyes opened because of a strong sense of pain. I could feel a prick in my foot, in the same foot that Durvasa had spared, the same spot that Barbarik had pierced. Before I could do anything a hunter came there and looking at me he feel down on his knees and asked for forgiveness—

" Lord, what is this sin that I have committed? I thought it was an animal, but it is your foot. Let me call the vaidya ."

I stopped him "You will not find any vaidya. What is your name?"

"Jara"

"Jara, remove the arrow and show it to me."

Under extreme pain I held the piece of the arrow. It was just like Aerak a piece of iron. Jara told me he found it in the stomach of some fish. Now I understood why Dau didn't ask the sage to lessen the curse. How would I have lived without him and the iron arrow had been made in my name. And now there was no point stopping what was bound to happen.

A few days back, I had sat right here and had said my farewell to Udhav, after telling him the Gita so that my words don't get lost and people who need them can find them. While explaining the story of life to Udhav there was another line of thought going on in my mind. I had to give this wisdom thrice, right before war. I gave it to Arjuna before the Mahabharata, told the Anu Gita before the Ashwamedha and Udhav Gita happened on it's own in Prabhas before the violence.

Now I wish I had told the Gita to my clan as well.

The violence could have been avoided. But the violence had never been delayed, I had on the name of Dharma shifted it to the larger ground. In the greed of saving my blood relations, if I would have delayed this struggle too on the basis of the Gita,Krishna would have been a lie and this detachment, yoga, the spread of this message where God and man, man and God become one would be declared a deceit. Either ways I had told Utang that all the positives were mine, my existence is in every form, truth and lies, sin and virtue, and whatever form I come in, I have to let the Dharma flow there.

Today I am waiting for departure.

Jara stayed with me and 3-4 days later Arjuna finally arrived. He told me that he met Daruk in the middle. Yudhisthira had seen a dream in which Dwarka was drowning and he had immediately sent Arjuna. I explained everything to Arjuna and told him to take the residents of Dwarka and told him to hug me. Arjuna hesitated, I asked him to hold my hand but he denied. I understood that someone had told him that if he touched me, I would take all his powers.

Without God humans will not be able to manage.

I told Arjuna to give me one side of the *Gandiva* and hold the other. He did that. It was true that from now on he had to live on his own. His entire life while being the son of Indra, he lived like a human, and me in my human form I became God. Who was whose strength was necessary to be established now. My Narayana form's powers were now gone. My actions that were seen as miracles were not just me, it had the vision of the scared people,for few it was the blind attachment, the greed for my love that gave birth to this. But today I was completely alone. God was alone.

There must have been a huge crowd of devotees but those that were pillars of strength they used to guide my path sometimes against my wishes. Behind the curtain of my divinity were the blessings of Dau and his sacrifice, Satyaki's presence around me, Daruk, my horses, my wives, and my shadows— Udhav and Chandhak. Chandhak used to worship me but he used to walk in front of me, making all arrangements for my safety as if their God couldn't take care of himself. Now all of them were gone.

My death was as normal as a human's but the area around me, created by me was Gods's. It is not very difficult but you need to have a willingness and the nature to stay connected with your surroundings. And for this, wanted or unwanted, important-unimportant wisdom collection is an art, so that when there is an opportunity you know more than the people around you. When you know more people around you, take you to be great, and then the path to divinity becomes shorter. Things you say today, according to math, can happen tomorrow, if not completely but parts of it. And when people believe what you say and do the same the future automatically turns fruitful and then becoming God is not very difficult.

What I call time is actually a humanly written future, people look for the future and the past in the stars. It is hard living in the moment because the present moment is detached, you are in it and there are stories, the stories that the human mind wants to believe, and that is the meaning of life. For others, everyone knows detachment but if a problem arises for self, then they take support from the past and worry about the future. This gives way to vicious needs and to get over them humans wrote Dharmshastras, even if they were wrong.They created sin and virtue, and other sources of strength just to keep each other in control. In the process to keep psychological control on each other, humans forget about themselves.

But a lot of people spread their generosity and get the strength to manage the lives of people weaker than them or the less wise. They try to be God by using their power and this is where their downfall starts.

To be above and beyond this illusion is to be Narayana.

To be Narayana is difficult for he lives in the instance and detached, being detached can lead to a swollen ego. When all the contradictions of good and bad, sin and virtue, past and future melt down in the thinnest slice of time Narayana emerges.

The instinctual nature decides the karma. Shiva knows everything, both important and the less important, but he never gets excited to jump into a situation till the fire doesn't reach him. And even then if words or boons suffice he wouldn't move. Shiva also rises above dharma and Adharma when it comes to creating the world through destruction.

And me. Dau used to say that if problems didn't find me then I found the problems and used to make everyone run. He was like Shiva. Both of them could see destruction with closed eyes. I used to get stuck in breaking and making. Hence, I had to say that I am the one who makes and I am the one who breaks. I did this so that people don't forget me and I keep the control on the happenings. And Shiva knew about my habit of keeping everything in control.

This time he had to change the Yuga. I don't know if he had decided this while playing dice with Gauri or was he disappointed with the present yuga. He played his turn and I came to know about this later. His change to the Yugas happened in the Universe and a small change was visible on earth. Other than me, he had put two other people at work, Shakuni and Duryodhana, both were the signs of change in demonic qualities, from Dwapar to Kaliyug.

Shakuni's entire family was killed by the Kaurava family by starving, after Gandhari's marriage..Daily grain supply was decreased for Shakuni and his brothers. In a few days the sons and the father understood that they cannot go on like this. Everyone started giving their grains to the wise Shakuni. One by one each of them died and their bodies were cremated in the prison

I was born in prison and Shakuni got a rebirth in one. I had not seen but lost my brothers before me ,he had seen his, die before his eyes. We never forgot each other, not even for a second, we were doing Shiva's work. My relationship with Shakuni was on some other level. I tried really hard to hide it but then one day it startled everyone. Someone had given the Pandavas a mirror by saying that they won't be able to see themselves. They will see the reflection of the person they love the most. Nobody wanted to come forward for the fear;of everything from the unconscious coming out and the fear of all dream castles crashing to the ground. What if all the beliefs, all love was false. Draupadi insisted— "Krishna, your consciousness and unconscious are the same, nothing is hidden, you look in this mirror." Everyone insisted. I tried to explain, I was not worried about my unconscious being revealed, I was scared about the hearts that would break. In that room everyone thought I loved them the most, every Krishnaa. I knew she wanted to see herself in the mirror with me, but I was worried that by seeing Radha in the mirror, she might feel bad.

But even I was shocked to look at the mirror, what was visible was not expected by anyone. There in the mirror was standing Shakuni. In a second everyone decided that the mirror was useless and false, because Krishna could not love Shakuni. The mirror was destroyed. Nobody asked me and I told nobody. The secret was that the mirror showed the person who was on your mind at that moment. The rest was not love or attachment.Who else would I think of other than Shakuni, in the play directed by Shiva we were the actors and were thinking about each other's moves. I had no idea about his sadness, but he was deeply hurt.

Firstly marrying his sister to a blind king and then death of his own in front of his eyes. When he was alone he was left by everyone. He kept wandering in the jungles, collecting powers and then he met Bhairav who taught him the dice and other tricks. The same trick that I knew, of negating myself and entering in someone else's. I was enlightened so I didn't keep my greed in the open, Shakuni was burning in the fire of revenge.

To know the mind of the person in front of you and to understand his thought process to change it is the way of the world. You don't need to look for the sky and heaven to be self made Gods. For this you have to be one with the living and the non living. You have to feel their thoughts inside you and this is where the danger starts. If one doesn't know the reaction or result of this then it only leads to ego and misuse. First the attainment of knowledge, then goodwill and then self recognition. After this being one with God, otherwise this power only leads to destruction. The greed and to think highly of oneself ends this majestic journey and sometimes it is in the hands of Ravana and Shakuni to destroy. God-Demon, Divine-Devil — the only apt path is between them with the right use of power. This game is about creating the world. It will go on from the Adikaal to the end, but what is the end ? It is a line moving both ways— straight and circular. Not everyone can follow the rules of this game and they get stuck.

In reality people don't see this as a game and they keep searching for the meaning and aim of life for their own sense of fear. As if finding the meaning will remove everything else. In the shadows of tradition, they hide their fear and their past— they live under the burden of the future. They think God will save all of them and he is looking at everyone very seriously. God in the whole universe is in a game, playing it only in the present, no meaning, just karma. The rest of the story is written to explain it to people. Play while the game is on, don't live in the moment, hear the inner voice, it will tell you the right move and rest everything is a pretence. You yourself will become god !! God just plays the right move at the right time, selflessly, beyond the concepts of winning or losing and even beyond feelings. When everything that is movable and immovable, fundamental and conscious, everything is at its position, that point in nature and the awake human mind that makes it possible, is completeness.

Shakuni would enter the mind of the opponent and the dice used to listen to him. Nobody else knew about this other than me that his dice were made by the bones of his father. In the air the speed and direction of these dice used to change in Shakuni's well practiced hands.

And then for his entire life he was there at the Kauravas, even after being insulted, he didn't meet his sister and neither gave the right advice to Duryodhana. The war could never have been averted.

Every chaotic and difficult line in the future that surrounds everyone starts at one point. That point was gambling, the game of power. Shiva's in the world and Shakuni's in Aryavarta. And that day I wasn't there to erase that point.

Shishupal's brother, Shalva, was causing havoc in Dwarka. I got stuck with that and here Yudhisthira in his greed for gambling. His defeat and the results were destined. By waging Draupadi he made a mistake. I had told Draupadi to always wear a yellow cloth inside. It was my colour and while disrobing when that colour came Bhishma stopped Dushasan. Everyone forgot Draupadi's question that day: how can a king who lost himself wage his queen. Draupadi got them their kingdom back as a boon against her insult from Dhritrashtra but the greed to play and win again gave them exile. Shakuni sowed the seeds of animosity and waited for me, so that an entire tree could grow.

Today my memory was making me hover over the earth like a hawk, above place and time from where everything was clearly visible. The arrow of time : from the past to the future. I was steady in mind and intellect for the first time like Shiva, immovable, still, just a viewer.

I closed my eyes and in one moment I saw a drowning Dwarka to Hastinapur, from Narkasur to Jarasandh, Rukmini and 16,000 women, my sons and everything that I did or I faced. Before my breath stopped on my mind were —Draupadi, Dau, Subhadra and my inner vision became still and focused on Radha. For some moments I stayed with Radha and she was eager to leave with me. I hadn't left the earth yet, I thought of breaking another rule, I kept doing this, but I never did it for myself. Today for myself I wanted to break a mental rule and behave like a human. Me, who in every moment could live in the smallest iota of time, was never burdened with the memory of the past and was never scared of the non-existent future. Today I was doing something for myself. While leaving the earth if I wanted to keep a memory from this life or this avatar as people say would not be of any war or Dharma. All of this will keep moving but what will not happen without me are the memories of my own being. That adventure is called - Raas.

Since the time I remember I have found myself surrounded by women. Dau and I were quite free under the nurturance of both the mothers. I don't remember the mischiefs from my crawling days but since childhood I have heard the story that someone told Yashoda maa that I ate mud and when she opened my mouth she saw the universe in it. But she remained a mother, she used to punish us but Rohini just gave us love. Love was in abundance, from young maidens to old women, all of them loved me with open hearts. When we started walking our courage increased and so did our mischief. Where people saw divinity in us, others saw love. Till the time we reached our adolescence, the definition of love had changed.The Gopis had left their motherly instincts and did not hesitate in showing their love. During childhood we used to break their pots and steal their butter. And all of them on the pretext of complaining used to come near us. The Gopis around me had become women but never changed their behaviour towards us.They used to fight like the Gopas, but those who were entering adolescence during our childhood, slightly older than us, were flowing in with some other feelings.

When Kama dev played his arrows no one knew. I was trying to catch the unconscious flow. And had all the time to fiddle with Kama. Other than herding the animals we started doing everything else. The Shastras, the art of weapons, music and dance (we played everything from the kumbh to the flute), seasons, the languages of the animals, all jobs from a cobbler to a farmer, from cooking meals to art, Dau and I left nothing. To do all of this our courage came from our independent thought and the rest was just rashness. The others were scared of the society and stayed behind us. We enjoyed it and they watched. In this, sometimes we even had to fight demons. But it never felt like it was a burden. Both of us were athletic and excelled in breaking boundaries. This affected the women, the fear they had from societal relations, and the irritation they had from being overpowered by men. They found a solution in Krishna and Balram.

The women were capable but I always wondered that in thousands of years, why did they behave like slaves. Maybe because in a power struggle with males, they were made to feel so but why did they believe in their inferiority. A marriage feels more like shackles and less of love. And life is spent in finding the moment to break free. But here the story was different. The women of Vrindavan were smart, my divine form showed them the way. They made their love for me their path of freedom like the Brahmin wives. One day while herding the cows we went a little far and hunger was on its peak. I told my friends to get food from the Brahmins. The Brahmins scolded them and told them to return. I told them to go to the Brahmin wives. As soon as they heard I was with them, they came with food for me even when the husbands stopped them from going. I was shocked to see their courage and I wanted to embrace them all but instead I said, "all of you return home, that is your dharma and duty. What will your husbands say?"

All of them said in unison, "Kanha, we heard that you help attain freedom and you are sending us back to dependence. We are aging while waiting for your love, no we don't want to go anywhere. If you reject us, like our husbands have rejected us, we will kill ourselves."

Their voices were so strong that I did not argue further. I embraced all of them and promised to accept them all mentally. That time they were all beyond physicality and were on a spiritual ground. A thread of attraction had surrounded all of us. This would have gone on if the others wouldn't have called out - "Kanhaiya, the Brahmins want to meet."

In front of me were standing their husbands, I started planning a verbal argument in my mind but desire had created needs here and doubt there. They had come to express guilt and ask for forgiveness. I quickly asked for the freedom of these women not from the household but from the mental slavery. The Brahmins agreed readily and taking me for God promised me. While going all the women left with mischievous smiles on their faces as if they were promising to meet again. I was in control but my friends couldn't stop laughing.

I had to make and keep a similar promise again. I had a game going on with a set of Gopis-- the game of love and love lorn struggles. The age to break their pots had gone. The wishes of youth and ego complement each other. In order to establish that they were out of my reach, they stopped paying attention to me. And I decided to teach them a lesson. It wasn't me it was the arrows of desire, but I had to draw a layer to the story. I found an opportunity very soon. One day a group of gopis were taking a bath before praying on the Yamuna bank without their clothes. When they were busy in the water, I stole their clothes from the bank and went and sat on the tree when they came out and didn't find their clothes. They were startled. They went back into the water and kept looking until one of them saw me.

" Kanha, what are you doing here ?"

" Why can't I come here ?"

" All of us are bathing."

"So"

"This is wrong. You can't look at us like this."

"I am not looking at you, I am playing the flute." After saying this I started playing the flute. All those maidens were stuck, in the madness of the flute and in the shame of nakedness.

" Kanha, our clothes are lost."

"Who took them, or did you come like this from home?"

"Save us, Kanha."

"Who am I to you ?"

Their voices became soft and turned into a plea. But this pleading was hidden in lust. In the evening, on the banks of Yamuna, on top of the Kadamba tree, in spring Krishna was being attacked by the arrows of kamadeva. Even I let it happen today.

" Come and take your clothes."

" How will we come, you come and return them."

" I won't come down, you will have to come."

"Please check if there is no one else."

I acted like I was checking.

The prettiest among them, who was also the bravest, came out, hiding her breasts with one arm and her thighs with the other. I was in the mood for mischief-- "get everyone."

Some of them came out, "a little more, a little more…", everytime I said that the mischief spread to them. Slowly they came nearer and now they weren't even trying to hide anything. All of them were near me and my body but I controlled my lust and did what I did with the Brahmin wives. I took their attention away from the body to the mind. We became one for a moment. And as soon as we calmed our passion, I told them to wear their clothes and made them believe that our love was beyond everything.They didn't want to leave me, but I promised that I would spend at least one entire night with them. And this did happen!

Among them some were very important to me and could talk about anything.This largely spread love was not everything. My life had another stream, which was beyond the games and was explaining to me the meaning of life, it was making me Krishna from Kanha. This stream was Radha.

I had a keen eye for beauty since childhood and in my

mischief I was never unfair with love but I was selfish when it came to being intimate in love. Vishaka and Lalita were very close to me, since childhood, beautiful, smart, just like Dau and I were together forever, the three of us were on a different level of love. But Radha was my desire, Vishakha and Lalita were the thread between us. When Radha and I were together ,this thread disappeared and when seperate they kept me bound. She was older to me, I was told but I never felt that, not even when we met for the first time. Yashoda Maa had tied me one day to a mortar, maybe then I used to crawl. Dau told me later that I had dragged it between 2 trees and put so much strength that the trees uprooted, maybe the trees were weak. But this story is from a time when I was older. Maa was very angry about the complaints she got about my stealing and destruction, Dau showed anger and escaped, but I was caught. Outside the house my mother tied me up and left, then I heard some noise outside. I knew very well that it would be Lalita. She was the one who used to instigate me to break the pots of the Gopis especially of the ones she didn't like. She used to give us the address and we used to enter their houses and eat all the butter and curd. Now I realise how hungry we were.

Anyways I was getting bored that day tied alone and I said - "Someone please untie me."Lalita came inside and smiled and sat beside me, but my mind was not on her, there was another girl with her. I kept looking at her. Fair, balanced figure, large eyes with no end, the air became scented, by the time she walked up to me, my eyes had become bigger. It felt like she and I were one, I didn't know about Ardhnarishwar then. Later when I heard this in the context of Shiva, I remembered that moment.

My stupor broke when Lalita snapped her fingers, Radha had vanished.

" Who was she ? where did she go ?"

" Kanha, while being tied you are dreaming. Look next to you."

Radha had come and was sitting beside me. I turned towards her and suddenly a flute started playing. She said "So you are the one who has troubled everyone."

" I didn't trouble you."

" I am beyond your reach."

"Till when?"

Lalita said "Kanha, you are meeting her for the first time, get to know her before fighting with her, she lives in Vrindavan, she is the daughter of Vrishbhan dada, Radha."

" I have heard it correctly, you do fight a lot. First you steal and then you make excuses."

Lalita dug her finger on my shoulder and said "But today the poor fellow…"

Before I could say anything bitter I felt a soft fingers in

my hair. I can't explain that feeling. Right now I wanted to get untied but after meeting Radha I wanted to stay tied forever. With eyes half closed I requested "Lalita please untie the rope, I won't fight again."

Radha said "Yashoda Maa has tied you and only she will untie you otherwise you will trouble the girls again. Let's go Lalita. I have to go across the river."

"Stay here Radha, I won't break your pots."

"If I stay here, you will forget everything" While she was saying this she slapped me lightly. At that moment Yashoda Maa came in. She saw Radha slapping me.

"Radha, your soft hands won't be able to control him. He is used to my scolding and slapping."

"Yashoda Maa let him go, he is in pain." Radha said this and left. While leaving she turned and blinked. Maa while untying me said "She will make a great wife and mother." What Maa thought was motherly instinct was actually going to start a completely different story.

Now my eyes kept looking for her and my mind was lost. Kamadev had instigated love way before time. Some years were spent playing and Radha had made a special spot and everywhere it was established that Radha kept me in control. I was not controlled but whenever Radha was around I didn't pay attention to anyone else. I had a different relationship with Radha and used to enjoy her company. My attraction for her was increasing day by day. I understood the reason for the same later when I had separated from her. I always had those people around me who used to say yes to me, I didn't get an ego because of my conscious mind. Only Dau used to say no but later he used to agree. Duryodhana didn't listen and only Radha said no to me .She used to even bring me to my knees to plead for her yes . When did this turn into love is unknown. Maybe when we were living in Vrindavan because of the fear from Kansa.

Vrindavan's forests, time and both of us. Everyone came to know. She used to listen to my flute for hours and I used to tie flowers in her hair. From putting red colour in her feet to managing clothes, our minds were one and our bodies weren't that far.

The leaves that shed from the trees were our bed, the branches used to save us from the sun, and Lalita and Vishakha were our bodyguards. They had given me to Radha without any jealousy. There was no tree in the forest that didn't know the touch of our bodies and who hadn't seen the beauty of Kama Shastra. We saw every change in our body together and got lost in them. I knew when Radha turned into a woman from a girl and she while running her hand in my hair had understood everything about me. Who will lose control in what moment both of us knew together.

In my ever moving life Radha was still, but social relations are so ruthless, and people scared.I came to know about this then. The fear of what people will say and behind this were the wrong impacts of caste and gender. These differences still divided life. Entire Vrindavan knew about our love but used to talk behind our backs. I used to get irritated by all these things but what would happen with that? I had to prove Radha right and pure, not like Rama who gave pain to Sita but by teaching society a lesson.

I just had to remember Kama deva, the fever arrows (jwara baan) defeated me as he was looking for an instance. My body was burning and all the doctors had failed. Father and Mother were distressed and that is when Sage Garg arrived. He knew every nerve of mine. He sent everyone outside and asked "What do you wish for, Lord."

" To cure my fever, sage."

" That will happen by your own wish, Lord."

In making me God his words and wanderlust were also involved. The sage had made me into a myth. I said something in his ear.

The sage went out and said- "Kanha's fever will be cured by one way, a pure maiden will walk on Yamuna and get water."

Nanda Baba announced it. The married women were out, the scared one ran away and the rest knew what had to be done. Yamuna was on a high tide, who would have walked on it. Dau and I knew it -- Radha on a dedicated time reached that spot where the water was the least deep and only Dau and I knew about this point. Here everyone had heard about it and some of them had reached the bank. Radha courageously put her foot down but there was no water, there was a rock that was helping Radha float.She only had to act as if she was walking. It was Dau's back that had the potential to carry land. Because of me Dau loved Radha. Radha was hesitant but he scolded her and said that he couldn't see a tear in either of our eyes. Even today Dau has Radha's footprints on his back. I had to later make Rewati Bhabhi understand.

As soon as they reached the bank, Dau vanished and Radha moved forward. Everything else was pre planned. As soon as my temperature came down, Maa Baba started to cry and kissed Radha. After some time Dau took the responsibility to drop Radha. I asked Sage Garg to stay back . Not only was her respect reinstated she had become a goddess in Gokul and Vrindavan. Either people are too naive or they just don't understand. But neither becoming a goddess or god helps you escape from the man made webs. I came to know about this in the next few days.

I told Yashoda maa- "You were showing love to Radha."

"She is so sweet."

"Then make her your daughter in law."

"Why?"She was shocked.

"Why ? Don't you know how much I love her."

"I know that but this marriage cannot happen."

"Why"

Maa said "Because she is older than you.She doesn't love you, just adores you."

"There is love. I love her and I will only marry her."

"This can't happen, she is Vrishbhan's daughter."

"So? Ask Baba to talk to him. He won't ignore his words."

"But she is different from our caste."

"I don't believe in all this."

" Even if you don't believe it, her marriage has been fixed with Ayan."

"Even after knowing that she is mine."

I was arguing with Maa when Baba entered. I threatened them that if Radha didn't come home they would lose their son too. Then what happened gave me the bitter taste of life. Tying people together was difficult,nobody could remove caste from God's mother. Sage Garg was called. After hours of arguments he told me that for the establishment of Dharma I was needed and how my life was going to be dangerous. Radha's life would have become unstable with me and I would never want that. My love for her didn't want to give her any pain. I dropped the idea to marry her and she got married to Ayan. But this didn't make any difference.

I revolted. Even Ayan knew that Radha was physically with him but mentally she was with me. Our love went on.The rest of the Gopis had got married but our love matured. I decided to break all societal relations, Dau either ways didn't worry about it. This reached its peak when it was decided that we would go to Mathura.Even we didn't know if we would return alive from Kansa's grip. We decided to do a MahaRaas. Smaller ones used to happen all the time when the Gopis would leave from their homes at night, then used to come and dance, sing and show love. All of them were scared but they couldn't stop themselves.I had taught all of them hypnosis.After making their husbands sleep they used to come and return before they woke up. But the MahaRaas was different, all the Gopis and Radha, Dau and I, all of us together, in one place for an entire night, only music and colours, sexual excitement, Kamadeva had full independence, fulfilling lust without any obstacles.

Lust had to be given shape that day, right now I think but that day it was pure happiness. But what happened was the opposite, the game Kama played with me was opposite to what he played with Shiva and Brahma. They were sitting in sacrifice, pulling them towards passion.I wanted to be in passion so he made me leave everything.

That night when Dau and I reached the forest, the moon had spread all its light and so did the Gopis' beauty. Excitement was dripping from their faces and their bodies. The entire forest was smelling of flowers and the natural beauty of the women. A few of them were hugging each other and some were touching. Some had their lips at other's cheeks. In one corner Radha was sitting explaining something. Maybe they were all looking for ways to make me get attached.

As soon as I arrived the Gopis hugged me as if they had been waiting since ages but my hunger was for something else. Radha did not get up. I stood against a tree and started playing the flute and Dau the Kumbh, slowly everyone started dancing. All the Gopis came around me, I was in the center.Some of them were next to me till the time someone removed them. I wanted to go near Radha but these women had tied me with their hands. Everything was in a trance and in order to touch me a small struggle had started. Whoever embraced me didn't want to leave me. Each one of them wanted to break all limits today, but the person I did this for was far away from me.

I thought I should make everyone happy. I slowly embraced everyone and left them in a trance.Everyone thought Krishna was with them. I walked towards Radha and she walked into the forest.I followed her but she did not stop. She moved ahead, turned, and put her arms around my neck. I carried her on my shoulder and made her sit on a rock while I kissed her feet. Radha put her fingers in my hair and I swayed my finger on her forehead. Radha kissed my forehead. For some moments Radha and Krishna became one, physically, from every inch. Before my lips touched hers we heard some noise. The Gopis had found us.

" Go, here come your lovers." Radha whispered in my ear.

"I had left them."

" When you leave Kanha, you want everything." She said "Go enjoy your heart's content, when you get tired, come, I will wait for you."

Kama shot the arrow of separation. She turned and left. For a second my ego awoke and I didn't call her. I turned and left with the Gopis. They had lifted me and were on the peak of drunkenness.It was going to be morning and nobody wanted to stay incomplete. I stayed all night but my mind had left with Radha. Before disappearing I turned and saw from behind the tree 2 eyes that were saying "I am here." My pain got lost in the tears from my eyes. And it remained embedded till today. What did I get ?

It took me some years to understand why the human mind is always distracted. The reason was just one.

It is said nature is in play, with humans and without it as well. The one who is God is also just a play, in war, in Raas, in lust. And Lust ? Who is exempt from it ? Brahma, Shiva or me? But I could control it with my unconscious mind and it became an illusion standing on his head. Illusion is a cloud of rumour that man takes to be reality. The Gods think they invented the illusion to keep man away from them and man takes this spiral web of illusions to be life. If man stays in doubt ,then God also gets stuck in it. Only I understood this because I had seen both the worlds.

Brahma in his isolation got excited and from his thoughts gave birth to Prajapati and Ashwini but went away. Brahma understood needs for the first time. Something new was born. One maiden, extremely beautiful, features so sharp that it was difficult to stop looking at her. For the first time in the universe a need arose and Brahma gave birth to Kama. After giving birth to Kama Dev the need to get that maiden arose and Brahma gave a boon to Kama Dev-

" I am giving you a boon, go and hit every man -- greed, doubt, craziness, anxiety, fever." And Kama hit his first arrow at Brahma. The birth of Lust happened in that moment and since then lust has made space and is going around in the world of humans, in the roots of everything. Illusion changes the form of lust. Brahma forgot everything and ran after that maiden. His sweat gave birth to the world, the maiden kept changing forms, Brahma became a man of different forms, Shatrupa was made. The vortex of lust surrounded everyone.Brahma got stuck in his own illusionary web, he couldn't think Kama was inciting these feelings from inside. To look at Shatrupa Brahma had made five faces. This running stopped when Shiva stopped him.

But he could not save himself either. He was sitting in meditation with his eyes closed, his awakening was necessary for the flow. Sati spread the web of beauty and needs and for I think but that day it was pure happiness. But what happened was the opposite, the game Kama played with me was opposite to what he played with Shiva and Brahma. They were sitting in sacrifice, pulling them towards passion.I wanted to be in passion so he made me leave everything.

That night when Dau and I reached the forest, the moon had spread all its light and so did the Gopis' beauty. Excitement was dripping from their faces and their bodies. The entire forest was smelling of flowers and the natural beauty of the women. A few of them were hugging each other and some were touching. Some had their lips at other's cheeks. In one corner Radha was sitting explaining something. Maybe they were all looking for ways to make me get attached.

As soon as I arrived the Gopis hugged me as if they had been waiting since ages but my hunger was for

something else. Radha did not get up. I stood against a tree and started playing the flute and Dau the Kumbh, slowly everyone started dancing. All the Gopis came around me, I was in the center.Some of them were next to me till the time someone removed them. I wanted to go near Radha but these women had tied me with their hands. Everything was in a trance and in order to touch me a small struggle had started. Whoever embraced me didn't want to leave me. Each one of them wanted to break all limits today, but the person I did this for was far away from me.

I thought I should make everyone happy. I slowly embraced everyone and left them in a trance.Everyone thought Krishna was with them. I walked towards Radha and she walked into the forest.I followed her but she did not stop. She moved ahead, turned, and put her arms around my neck. I carried her on my shoulder and made her sit on a rock while I kissed her feet. Radha put her fingers in my hair and I swayed my finger on her forehead. Radha kissed my forehead. For some moments Radha and Krishna became one, physically, from every inch. Before my lips touched hers we heard some noise. The Gopis had found us.

" Go, here come your lovers." Radha whispered in my ear.

"I had left them."

" When you leave Kanha, you want everything." She said "Go enjoy your heart's content, when you get tired, come, I will wait for you."

Kama shot the arrow of separation. She turned and left. For a second my ego awoke and I didn't call her. I turned and left with the Gopis. They had lifted me and were on the peak of drunkenness.It was going to be morning and nobody wanted to stay incomplete. I stayed all night but my mind had left with Radha. Before disappearing I turned and saw from behind the tree 2 eyes that were saying "I am here." My pain got lost in the tears from my eyes. And it remained embedded till today. What did I get ?

It took me some years to understand why the human mind is always distracted. The reason was just one.

It is said nature is in play, with humans and without it as well. The one who is God is also just a play, in war, in Raas, in lust. And Lust ? Who is exempt from it ? Brahma, Shiva or me? But I could control it with my unconscious mind and it became an illusion standing on his head. Illusion is a cloud of rumour that man takes to be reality. The Gods think they invented the illusion to keep man away from them and man takes this spiral web of illusions to be life. If man stays in doubt ,then God also gets stuck in it. Only I understood this because I had seen both the worlds.

Brahma in his isolation got excited and from his thoughts gave birth to Prajapati and Ashwini but went away. Brahma understood needs for the first time. Something new was born. One maiden, extremely beautiful, features so sharp that it was difficult to stop looking at her. For the first time in the universe a need arose and Brahma gave birth to Kama. After giving birth to Kama Dev the need to get that maiden arose and Brahma gave a boon to Kama Dev-

" I am giving you a boon, go and hit every man -- greed, doubt, craziness, anxiety, fever." And Kama hit his first arrow at Brahma. The birth of Lust happened in that moment and since then lust has made space and is going around in the world of humans, in the roots of everything. Illusion changes the form of lust. Brahma forgot everything and ran after that maiden. His sweat gave birth to the world, the maiden kept changing forms, Brahma became a man of different forms, Shatrupa was made. The vortex of lust surrounded everyone.Brahma got stuck in his own illusionary web, he couldn't think Kama was inciting these feelings from inside. To look at Shatrupa Brahma had made five faces. This running stopped when Shiva stopped him.

But he could not save himself either.He was sitting in meditation with his eyes closed, his awakening was necessary for the flow. Sati spread the web of beauty and needs and for one moment Shiva opened his eyes. Kama Dev's arrow hit him in that span. Lost, Shiva got lost in beauty. Music, flowers, dance, love-- Shiva the meditative got lost in human-like behaviour. Even he didn't know what he was doing.

The world is also very similarly made and broken, with wants, struggles, events, accidents. Hope-despair, life-death everything is tied with this thread of want and of lust. I knew all of this but nobody could be spared from Kama's arrows. But I was enjoying this illusion, the conscious mind wanted to answer so I did it through Raas which was the shaping of desire into love.But I didn't get the time to think if it actually happened.

If the voice hadn't come I would have kept thinking if this was a mental thought or the truth, my body was here and I was there.

"Let's go"- I turned and saw a hand moving towards me. It was Shiva.

Before holding his hand I started laughing, even though he was smiling. Both of us were smiling at the same thing. A few years ago, both of us were standing in front of each other, ready to fight. It was neither his war nor mine, but time had brought friends against each other. He was there for his devotee Banasur and I was there for my great-grandson Anirudh who had been captured by Banasur because he wasn't letting his daughter marry him.

In actuality my mind was not attached to anyone, but I had some different parts as well- my conch "Panchjanya", My bow "Sarang", all the weapons and Sudarshan Chakra, my chariot "Jaitra" and "Garuddhwaj", Daruk and my horses- Meghpushp, Shaviya, Sugriv, Baalhak-- that day in war Shiva had made me sacrifice everything along with all my tricks and ego about myself. Then both of us took out biological weapons, I took out the Vaishnava and Shiva took out Maheshwar.There was despair all around because these biological weapons left an impact for hundreds of years. We stopped and did not unleash the biological arrows.

It was a play without a feeling of envy or animosity but I had taken a promise from Shiva, that the day I will want to leave everything he will help me.

I held Shiva's hand and left to look for rest.

It is said rebirth happens with a load of destiny (*prarabdh*), that forms the inner self or natural behaviour, but in the entire world only humans can change it through decision and action (*Purushartha*). Is it true ?or has this been told to keep humans busy. Because I had to come to earth in many forms, every form had limited powers and capabilities but the reason was the same-- to establish Dharma. From a fish to Krishna, I covered a journey from water to land over lakhs of years. But in every Yuga, Dharma and truth are in danger. Like Parushuram I soiled the land with blood, like Rama followed the modesty and I have already told you the story of this birth.

Now I don't want to ask Shiva anything further and give him any trouble. If I have to return I will try and go beyond the struggles. Desire gives birth to sadness, look at it and don't go after it. Maybe this might change humanity -- I will have to become Buddha if it goes on like this, and I will have to live in contradictions because I will be sent for protecting Dharma but Dharma itself will stand on one leg in Kaliyuga.From Treta to Dwapar to Kali --will a Kalki Avatar save everything. Earlier only the ruler was corrupt and the people were in pain but the ruler took care of them. In Kaliyug every man would be corrupt, Arjunas will ask questions but before the answer will change sides, the ruler will only fulfill his ego and people will take survival in daily life to be a blessing. I have started it. Dharma was in danger but I could not save it. Maybe I will have to come -- for complete destruction.

But my experience is saying all of this, I gave all my love

as well, maybe I will have to come for complete love. And this did happen. I haven't come back from my body. I am forced to come for love, in people's minds.Mostly people call me when they are in unbearable pain or when they are in fear.But there was one moment when I had to travel in a human form.It felt like a box of time where the Gopis and Gopas had come to earth this time with devotion.No fear, no hopes just love.

Surdas, Raskhan and Meera. I had to show different forms to them. People say that I give too much trouble and only then I come. I am used to giving sadness to people. If you find the Gopis they will tell you the same.

My devotees will say the same.But I don't want to give pain, people understand it as pain. I just pull on some emotional strings and I want their heart to be excited before their minds when they actually meet me. When pain or happiness is on the peak is when meeting others is a pleasure. Otherwise the energy is wasted.

People get stuck in right and wrong and pay more attention to momentary impulse and get stuck on the path itself. But Meera looks at the destination, receives troubles, cries - she leaves everything but never leaves me. I had to come, not even the Gopis had done something like this. In the inner corners of her mind the Krishna that Meera had made was not just an idol, it had become her existence and identity. Just like Surdas who had filled so much love in my child form that there was no way I could have shown him the adult Krishna.

Even today if someone wants, I can come. Without any bets. How you want to call me is your decision.

■■

About the Author

Dr. Alok Bajpai

Dr. Alok Bajpai is a Psychiatrist trained at NIMHANS, Bangalore, presently working at Kanpur after few stints abroad. Apart from practicing Psychiatry, a consistent focus of his work is with children, adolescent and youth, while being associated with various Institutes and schools. His work extends beyond the confines of clinic into freelance teaching of mental health issues and life skills. Psychiatry, Physics, Film, Music, Literature and Teaching are only some of the things that occupy Dr. Alok Bajpai's wide world. He has been instrumental in putting together many awareness campaigns and workshops - especially with schools and has trained teachers - aiming at increasing sensitivity towards childhood problems, in many Indian cities. These interactions are directed especially to the process of critical thinking, as an attempt of brain training to help the young minds evolve and evaluate their own ideology. He is also a regular columnist who writes about issues of mental health and socio-politics of life.

One special passion with Alok is the transformational process of the mind to enhance inner harmony and peace as Mahatma Gandhi remains his leitmotif and example. He is the curator of an interactive programme 'An Hour with the Mahatma' focussing on the transformative skills of Mahatma Gandhi. Gandhi for him is the tool to improve life skills and his exploration continues in applying Gandhi's tools to various walks of life especially conflict resolution and compassion.

He is also a Cinema student and left his busy schedule to attend the FTII - film appreciation course at Pune and did similar courses in Australia. He conducts Film Appreciation courses for students too.

He is engaged in interdisciplinary research at IIT and has few publications in Scientific reports (Nature), exploring Brain processes. His MOOC courses on NPTEL – 'Psychiatry An Overview' and 'How the Brain creates mind' are popular.

He can be reached at alokbajp@gmail.com

About the Illustrator

Pranoy Basak

An illustrator and visual designer, who likes to combine art with design whenever possible - he finds himself both an artisrt and a designer.

Having done his Bachelors in Design from UID (Unitedworld Institute of Design) in the field of Visual Communication, he always looks for things that excite him and when necessary, ready to explore new things.

Born in Chandannagar, West Bengal, his hometown is in Kanpur, Uttar Pradesh; and that makes him a cool Bengali with a tinge of "*Kanpuriya*".

Apart from illustrating and coming up wih visual solutions to problems, he's an equally passionate musician mostly as a keyboardist / pianist. He's a car as well as a commercial aviation enthusiast, and some other interests of him include, Formula 1, cricket, the paranormal, spirituality, photography, reading and occassional writing.

He can be reached through mail - basakpranoy97@gmail.com

and through his instagram account - @udi_babaaa

He can also be contacted though his Linkedin account - Pranoy Basak.

More of his works on visual design and illustration can be viewed on his Behance profile - behance.net/basakpranoy/

About the Editor / Translator

Ishita Sehgal

Ishita did her Bachelor of Arts in English from Ashoka University, India and her MPhil in Gender Studies from Trinity College, Dublin. She is interested in Mythology and has researched on the Mahabharata and Ramayana from a feminist context for her research. Her papers explore the evolution of women in society as viewed by cinema and other visual mediums. She has assisted in the making of a documentary at IIT Kanpur and taught as a teaching fellow at Ashoka University. Currently, she is pursuing her Ph.D. in English from Indiana University, Bloomington.Her research interests lie in Graphic Novels, Visual Literature and Ekphrasis. She is particularly inquisitive about the gutters, blank spaces and how we form our identity and memory from these spaces. Her questions of displacement and belonging are deeply influenced by colors and narratives of the graphic literature. In her fun time , she likes to read, travel , write and is a trained professional Bharatanatyam Dancer. She can be reached at - ishisehgal@gmail.com

From Text to Visual :

Visual development of Krishna

As metioned earlier, Krishna has to be shown as a human. As a result of the research conducted in the section of "Physical atributions of Krishna", the skin colour of Krishna has been kept more "human-like" and dark rather than the blue colour in which he is most commonly seen. Other attributions include the flute and the peacock feather. An overall attempt is to show Krishna "less divine" and "more human".

Initial sketches -

Coloured sketches -